NEIL HUNTER

TWO FROM TEXAS

Complete and Unabridged

LINFORD
Leicester

First published in Great Britain in 2014

First Linford Edition
published 2016

A catalogue record for this book is available
from the British Library.

ISBN 978–1–4448–2935–8

Published by
F. A. Thorpe (Publishing)
Anstey, Leicestershire

Set by Words & Graphics Ltd.
Anstey, Leicestershire
Printed and bound in Great Britain by
T. J. International Ltd., Padstow, Cornwall

This book is printed on acid-free paper

TWO FROM TEXAS

One of the men arrives in Gunner Creek at the end of a long search, whilst the other simply drifts into the town. Fate has drawn them together: two Texans who find a town in trouble — and, being who they are, have to throw in their hands to help. Chet Ballard and Jess McCall are Texicans down to the tips of their boots. Big men with hard fists and fast guns, who see trouble and refuse to back away from it . . .

1

Jess McCall, all six foot six inches, left the King High saloon without touching the ground. The batwing doors crashed open as his one hundred and eighty pounds catapulted through. McCall made an awe-inspiring sight as he sailed over the boardwalk. He landed hard, with a thump that rocked the building he had just left. Dust billowed up around his body as he slid into the middle of the wide, sun-baked main street of Gunner Creek, Territory of Kansas.

McCall climbed to his feet and tried to rid himself of the coat of gray-white dust that had settled on him. He managed to half-choke himself when he attempted to brush it off. He gave up when, on glancing up, he saw on the saloon steps the three bouncers who had just thrown him out. A loud snort of anger came from his throat as he made for them. They, seeing his intention, moved down the steps.

Though it was early, only ten in the morning, a fair-sized crowd was rapidly gathering.

McCall's opponents seemed pleased with the crowd, as though they wanted plenty of spectators. They also seemed confident and relaxed. As if this sort of thing happened often.

For a few seconds the men, in the center of the dusty circle made by the crowd, eyed one another. McCall stood motionless, his arms at his sides, feet spread wide apart for balance

Then the center one of the three bouncers moved forward. He was a big, solidly-built man, with a thick chest, long arms and huge fists. His name was Ed Quince. His beefy face was rough and bore the marks of a seasoned saloon brawler. Just before he had been thrown out, McCall, in an attempt to lessen the odds, had landed a single blow on Quince's face. Now a big purple and blue bruise was forming on Quince's left cheek. Mute testimony to the power of the McCall fist.

McCall tried to keep one eye on the advancing Quince, and also watch the moves of his partners. He only got a pair of aching eyeballs for his efforts. He did, however, get a glimpse of the two as they split up. One going to the left, the other to the right. Then his range of vision was greatly reduced by Quince's vast bulk.

Quince stood before McCall, his great fists clenching and unclenching. He said, 'Bucko, I'm going to split you in two.' He was, by nature, a man of few words.

Without giving Quince time to carry cut his threat, McCall drew back his right arm. It slashed forward again and his fist slammed into Quince's stomach with crippling force. Quince's small eyes shot wide open, his mouth forming a round O as his breath left his body in a rush. McCall flinched back from the gust of whisky-stale air. As Quince buckled forward, clutching his stomach, McCall swung his right again; this time it came hard and fast from his shoulder, a punch that ended on Quince's unshaven jaw with a crack that was heard by every man in the crowd. It dropped Quince like a sack of potatoes.

A moving shadow on the ground made McCall swing round fast. The owner was one of the other bouncers, a tall hulk of a man called Pink. Before McCall could complete his turn, Pink stepped in close. A ham-sized fist caught McCall a solid thump on the side of the head. The blow sent the Texan reeling, his arms flailing as he tried to keep his balance. Pink kept swinging as he followed McCall's weaving body. Then McCall's feet went from under him and he fell. Swift to make the most of an offered opportunity, Pink rushed in, launching a powerful kick. McCall rolled clear of Pink's booted feet. Clouds of dust followed in his wake as he spun himself across the ground.

Coming to his feet, McCall was able to meet Pink as the bouncer came at him.

Behind Pink was the third bouncer, and McCall saw a chance to end the thing fast. Lowering his head, McCall launched himself forward at Pink. The top of McCall's head slammed into Pink's stomach, the force of the blow sending Pink back into a collision with the third bouncer. As the two men crashed to the ground in a tangled heap McCall moved in. He grasped hold of them by the fronts of their shirts and swung them together. Two heads slammed together with a loud crack. McCall released the two and they dropped to the ground and lay still.

McCall drew in a deep breath and shook his head. His body ached and his head rang, but apart from that he felt fine. He glanced at the two still forms on the ground and grinned.

Then the grin left his lips as a voice cracked the hot silence.

'I'm ending this now, Bucko,' said Quince.

McCall turned in the direction of the voice and saw Quince standing near the saloon steps. Quince's right hand hovered over the butt of his tied-down .44. Blood ran from his lower lip and dripped onto his shirt.

From somewhere in the crowd a man shouted, '*He's got no gun.*'

Quince grinned at that. His head moved back and forth as he scanned the faces of the crowd. The low murmur of voices died away under his gaze.

'Maybe one of you wants to lend him one?' he said.

Nobody spoke up, or moved and McCall, despite the heat, felt a knot of ice-cold fear twist his stomach. He wasn't afraid to die, but this way was no way to go, being gunned down like some stray dog. It seemed that not a man in the crowd had the guts to stand up to Quince, even though it meant seeing a man shot down without a chance. McCall saw some of the men look away as he glanced at them. But he found he had more pity than hate for them.

Quince was still grinning. 'Looks like you ain't gettin' a gun, big man,' he said. His hand began a slow, deliberate move towards his own sidearm.

He's waiting for me to beg or run, McCall thought.

Then suddenly a man pushed his way to the front of the crowd. Out of the corner of his eye, McCall saw the man, and as McCall saw him, the man called, '*Hey, cowboy.*'

McCall cocked his head in the man's direction and saw the rifle the man held. In that instant the man swung the rifle up and tossed it in McCall's direction. McCall's hands came up and he caught the rifle. His right hand was working the lever as he swung the gun round to bear on Quince.

Quince saw McCall's move and his hand speedily yanked his gun from its holster. His face was a mask of surprise and anger.

As McCall's finger curled around the rifle's trigger he dropped to one knee.

Then Quince had his gun out and it blossomed flame at McCall. The slug tore into the ground close to McCall's left heel, sending up a geyser of dirt as it struck.

Before Quince could fire again, the rifle in McCall's hands rose, and he triggered off his first shot. The rifle was a 44–40 Winchester, and the heavy slug slammed into Quince's left shoulder. Off balance, Quince tried to sight his gun again.

As he saw Quince trying for a second shot McCall let go a second and third slug from the Winchester.

Quince took both slugs in the chest and the force of them slammed him backwards. He came up against the railing that edged the boardwalk and hung motionless for a moment. Then he slithered loosely along the railing until he fell face down in the dust of the street. His back was a blood-soaked mess of torn flesh and cloth where the rifle slugs had ripped their way right through his body.

The deep rumble of gunfire still echoed in the hot air as the crowd began to find their voices again. Slowly at first, then faster, they moved forward, pushed closer now the danger was over. All of a sudden they were men again as they surged towards the body of Quince. No longer afraid of the man who had made them back down scant minutes before.

Jess McCall shoved his way free of the crowd, not too gently for he was angry that this thing had happened. But, he realized, it was the way of things out here. A small thing, like a few wrong words and a man could find himself in deep trouble. And nine times out of ten the matter would be settled by the roar of guns and the spilling of blood. McCall gave a shake of his head.

He was brought out of his dark thoughts by a deep voice that asked, 'Finished with it, friend?'

McCall glanced up. Standing before

him was a big, dark haired man in sun-bleached, dusty clothing. The man was McCall's height and weight. He wore a tied down Colt .45 strapped to his right leg.

'Nice gun,' McCall remarked as he returned the Winchester. He smiled. 'I sure do thank you. It looked like my time was up before you stepped in.'

The man held out a big hand. 'Ballard is the name. Chet Ballard.'

McCall took the offered hand in his own large fist. 'Jess McCall,' he said.

'Howdy, Jess,' Ballard said.

They moved away from the crowd of men and walked slowly across the street.

'You had breakfast yet?' McCall asked suddenly. Ballard shook his head and McCall said, 'Me neither. Let's go get some.'

2

From a window two floors above the King High saloon a man's face drew back from the glass. The window overlooked the main street and the man had watched the incident below with detached interest. Now, however, he jerked away from the window as if the glass had suddenly become hot.

The man was Wade Temple, owner of the King High. A self-styled man of many, and ever-changing, moods and ideas. But he was a dangerous man too because of his inability to control his emotions. In Gunner Creek he was the hand that held the reins of command over a crew of hired gunmen who, in turn, ran the town the way Temple wanted it run.

Since his coming to the town, a year ago, he had worked his way up to his present position by the sheer brutality and violence his crew wielded. His reason, his objective for all this was one thing.

Money.

The rigged gambling tables in his saloon brought in a great deal. But Temple wanted more. So his men collected more from the town's storekeepers. They used the old, and well-tried *protection insurance*, by which the storekeepers paid to have their stores protected against non-existing accidents.

At first the townsfolk resented Temple's rule. But after a couple of men had been badly beaten up and one store almost destroyed they knuckled under. They paid up rather than risk being set on by Temple's vicious crew.

So a town was broken by a man who lived and cared for only one thing. A man who would go to any lengths to reach his goal. Someone who had no thoughts or worries about what he was doing to a town and its people.

Wade Temple didn't give a damn

about anyone. So long as his wealth was accumulating he lived in a world of his own creation. A world he had built when he was a child to blot out the picture of his squalid home life. And ever since that childhood, living in a stinking sod hut on the bank of the Mississippi, when he had sworn to better himself, the lust for the finer things in life had driven him to desperate measures to obtain them. From petty thieving in his teens, his desire for greater gains had set him on an insatiable trail of stealing and cheating. And in some cases killing. He had carried his dealings into the war by turning to gun running, and after had traded the weapons to hostile Indians from Arizona to Texas.

The army had finally broken up his gun running after a Texas rancher named Jack Halstrom had stumbled on one of Temple's rendezvous points and alerted the nearest cavalry post. After a running fight, Temple, and his second in command, a hard case gunslinger named Rio, were the only ones to escape. And before they left Texas they paid a visit to the Halstrom ranch. When they rode out they left Halstrom, his wife, and young son dead.

They also left for dead a man by the name of Chet Ballard.

Ballard had been a deputy in the small town where Temple ran his gun running from. Temple hated him. His hate for Ballard came from an incident that had taken place one hot day. Ballard had been arresting one of Temple's men for attacking a young girl. After talking had failed, Temple tried to get his man off by bribing the Texan. The bribe failed too. And Ballard had dragged Temple out into the middle of town and given him the biggest beating he'd ever had, with most of the town watching.

Temple had never forgotten the beating, and when he had seen Ballard at Halstrom's ranch that day he had gunned the Texan down without hesitation.

The incident had drifted into the past as Temple and Rio had moved around the country in the following couple of years. Then they had come on Gunner Creek. A small, one street town, way out in the empty vastness of Kansas. It lay in a wide sweeping valley that gave it ample protection from severe weather conditions. And the town was ringed by a number of ranches and farms.

Wade Temple had moved in and brought hired guns to do his work for him while he sat back and played king.

But suddenly, without warning his kingdom lost some of its glamour and the foundations crumbled a little. Out of his past came someone who could cause his downfall. Or his death.

Temple's handsome face became pale beneath its tan. He crossed from the window of his office and sat down behind his huge oak desk.

He was a tall, well-built man. His carefully groomed hair was fair. So was the neat mustache he wore on his upper lip. The clothes he wore were expensive and stylish, his boots hand stitched, the leather embossed.

Now he sat staring down at the highly polished surface of the desktop. He ran a trembling hand through his thick hair. Then he gave a groan and slammed his fists down onto the desk, hard.

'Damn you, Ballard,' he said softly. 'Damn you.'

Abruptly he raised his head and shouted: '*Rio, get in here*!'

Footsteps sounded beyond the office door, then it opened and a man came in. He closed the door and looked at Temple curiously as he crossed over to the desk.

Rio was a lean, sun-darkened man dressed in somber black from head to foot. His face was hard, and the skin was drawn tight over the bones of his face giving him a wasted, gaunt appearance. From behind half-closed lids his eyes settled unwaveringly on Temple.

'What the hell is up with you?

Somebody steal your damn safe?' he asked dryly.

'Don't be smart,' Temple snapped. 'It doesn't suit you.'

Rio's reply was a faint smile, more a sneer, that tugged at the corners of his thin lips.

'So what do you want?' he asked.

Temple rose from his seat and led the way back to the window. Rio followed him and peered through the glass.

'You see the two men walking across the street?' he asked.

'Yeah.'

'Take a close look at the one with the rifle.'

'*So?*' Rio asked after a second or so.

'Recognize him?'

'Should I?'

'Yes.'

'Come on then. Why?'

'Because he happens to be Chet Ballard,' Temple said, turning away from the window.

Rio leaned forward and studied the figure. Then he gave a dry chuckle.

'Hell, it is Ballard! How'd that son turn up here?'

He turned from the window and shook his head at Temple.

'You sure did kill him good,' he said. And there was an edge of contempt in his tone.

He glanced out the window again in time to see Ballard and his companion entering the Bonanza Restaurant on the other side of the street. On turning back into the office Rio saw Temple standing behind his desk. Temple was thumbing shells into a .44 Remington revolver.

'Think you'll need that?' Rio asked. He seemed amused at Temple's obvious nervousness.

Temple looked up sharply, his smooth features twisted into a dark scowl. He finished loading the gun and lifted a rolled gun-rig from an open drawer in his desk. He strapped it on before he spoke.

'Ballard didn't come to Gunner Creek by chance. He came because he knows we're here.'

'And you reckon he's going to come looking for us?' Rio said softly.

'Wouldn't you if you were in his place?' Temple asked.

Rio perched himself on the edge of Temple's desk. He watched Temple drop the loaded Remington into its holster. He knew the reason for Temple's fear. In the long time they had been together it had always been Rio who did the gunning. The simple explanation for this was in the fact that Temple was no use as a gun hand. For one thing he didn't have the nerve, for another he was too slow. Oh, he could plan and organize an operation with ease and speed. But come any gunplay and Temple was out. If he ever had to face up to a man in a fair fight he would panic and run. This, Rio knew without ever having seen it. *Hell,* he thought, *one look at Ballard and the bastard is ready to go underground.*

In answer to Temple's question, Rio

said, 'If it were me, I guess I would use a gun. But Ballard is a thinking man. He's got brains and he'll use them. He'll make us sweat, let us worry until we don't know what we're doing. Then he'll let us make the mistakes so we fall right where he wants us to.' Rio shrugged his shoulders. 'That's only *my* opinion. I could be wrong.'

'I don't think you are,' Temple said. 'Maybe we ought to move first. Get rid of him fast. I've got enough worry with this trail end town. I don't want to get tangled up with a Texas saddle tramp who has a grudge against me.'

'Okay,' Rio said. 'Leave it to me. I'd like to work on it my way.'

Temple nodded. 'Suit yourself, Rio. But do something soon.'

Rio slid off the desk and crossed to an oak cabinet that held a few bottles of whisky. He picked up a glass and poured himself a drink.

Temple went back to the window. He was conscious of the gun-rig around his waist and the heavy pull of the gun on his thigh. He hoped desperately that he would never have to use the weapon.

He forced himself to look down on the crowd who still milled about the body. Standing over Quince was the town's sheriff, Ernie Peckard, an old timer who was just the kind of lawman that Temple could tolerate. A man who was too old and weak to do anything that could harm Temple.

As Temple gazed down into the street he saw without paying due notice, a figure crossing the street. The man's name was Dicken Hodges, a one-time buffalo hunter who spent most of his time now in the town's saloons. But at the moment the man was hurrying across the street, carrying a pair of saddlebags and a battered hat. He mounted the boardwalk and went into the Bonanza restaurant.

Then Temple's mind turned to other matters and he left the window and crossed to his desk. Had he stayed he would have seen two men carry Quince off to the undertaker's parlor. He would have also seen Ernie Peckard leave the dispersing crowd and make his way slowly across the street and head for the Bonanza Restaurant.

3

As McCall followed Ballard into the restaurant he glanced back over his shoulder. The crowd had, if anything, become larger. McCall saw the bouncer called Pink, and his partner, crawl from beneath the feet of the crowd. The two staggered to their feet. Supporting each other they made their unsteady way inside the King High.

McCall continued on into the cool, clean interior of the restaurant. The place was deserted, though a good few of the tables held partly eaten meals.

'You sure do have a good way of clearing a place,' Ballard said.

McCall grinned. He joined Ballard at an empty table. He glanced over towards the counter and the curtained doorway that obviously led to the kitchen.

'Hey! Anybody home?' he called. To

Ballard he said, 'I hope they ain't gone far. I'm damn near fading away. I ain't eaten in nearly two days.'

'No time?'

'No money,' McCall said.

Ballard gave a loud laugh at McCall's dour tone.

'What started all the fuss back there?'

McCall growled, 'All over a damn game of poker.'

'You winning?'

'Yeah.'

'And?'

McCall shrugged his massive shoulders. 'You know what these saloons are. If they're winning everything's all right. But let a feller take some of their money and they get sore. I'd played a good game with the house and won a roll. We'd played most all night. So I decided to quit. But the dealer got nasty. When I tried to leave he called in reinforcements.' McCall grinned. 'That's when I made my big entrance.'

'How much did you win?' Ballard asked.

'Reckon it was about six or seven hundred. Hell, I had to borrow five bucks off an old feller I met to get in the game.'

At that moment Dicken Hodges came into the restaurant. Spotting McCall he gave a shrill yell as he came over to the table.

'Hey, you sure do hop around some, feller,' he said.

'That's me,' McCall said.

Hodges slid into chair. He dropped the saddlebags he was carrying onto the floor. Then he handed McCall the battered hat he held.

'You kind of left in such a hurry you forgot your stuff,' Hodges said.

He shoved a leathery hand down the front of the greasy buckskin shirt and drew out a roll of banknotes, handing it over. McCall held the roll in front of his face.

'Son,' he said, 'take a long look at that because it will be a hell of a time before you see another roll like it.'

Hodges gave a dry chuckle. He said,

'That card player tried to grab it when they tossed you out. I give him a whack on the head with a bottle and got out by a side window.'

McCall pulled a few notes from the roll and thrust them into Hodges' hand. The old man stared at the money.

'Hey,' he said, 'I only lent you five. There's more than that here.'

'You earned it, feller,' McCall told him.

Hodges grinned all over his brown face as he stuffed the money down the front of his shirt.

'Who's your friend?' he asked, glancing at Ballard.

McCall introduced the two men. Hodges nodded hello, then asked, 'You from Texas too?'

Ballard nodded. 'Place called Duckett.'

McCall asked, 'Think you could find the owner of this place before I waste away?'

Hodges got up. 'Sure thing.' He moved swiftly across the restaurant floor. Going behind the counter he pushed through the curtained doorway.

'You down here special?' Ballard asked.

'No,' McCall replied, 'I just drifted this way from Colorado. How about you?'

'I got reasons,' Ballard said gently.

Before either of them could say more a shadow fell across the table. McCall glanced up and saw a tall, lean, deeply tanned man. He wore a silver star on his faded shirt. He was an old man, thick white hair and a neat white mustache that stood out vividly against his brown skin. His eyes, of blue, a pale, piercing blue, were fixed unwaveringly on McCall. He was Ernie Peckard.

'Morning, Sheriff,' McCall said as Peckard sat down.

'Reckon you know why I'm here?' he said. His voice was dry and soft. The well-trained voice of a man who would never betray his emotions by the tone of his voice. 'It's only routine. I saw the whole thing from my office.' He glanced towards Ballard. 'That was a pretty smart move, mister. Glad to see someone in this town with a few guts.'

'Call it my good deed for the day,' Ballard said lightly.

Peckard nodded. 'When you've eaten, come over to my office and I'll take statements for the records.'

McCall glanced at Ballard, who nodded. 'We'll be there,' McCall told him. 'Sheriff, I'm sorry it had to happen. He gave me no choice.'

'Don't be sorry,' Peckard said. 'Quince had been heading for it a long time.'

'Don't take offence, Sheriff,' Ballard said, 'but I can't help thinking that maybe this town doesn't deserve what McCall did. Hell, not one man in that crowd made a move to help when Quince went for his gun.'

Peckard sighed deeply. He pulled off his hat and placed it on the table, staring at it for a time.

'This is only a small town we've got

here,' he said. 'The people who live around here are either ranchers or farmers. They can plant corn or brand a steer, but when it comes to bracing a hired gun, well, it's a little out of their line.'

'Who did Quince work for, Sheriff?' McCall asked.

Peckard glanced at him. 'I forgot you fellers are new in town,' he said.

'Would his name be Wade Temple?' Ballard asked. Peckard nodded, and the Texan's face hardened, his jaw muscles bunching tightly.

The old lawman studied Ballard for a few seconds then asked, 'You know him from somewhere?'

'Texas,' Ballard replied. 'Been looking for him a couple of years. Now I've found him.'

'Can you tell me?'

'Temple and his sidekick, Rio, killed a family I knew. I stopped a couple of slugs myself. It laid me up for a few months.'

Ballard outlined the story for Peckard

and McCall. He talked softly. But he was not able to keep hidden all of the deep feeling he carried inside him. When Ballard finished there was a moment of silence around the table.

'A man must be pretty low to go round killing kids,' McCall said.

'It fits his character,' Peckard said. 'Anything hurts him, he'll get even no matter what.'

Briefly, the lawman described Temple's position in Gunner Creek.

'Like I said before,' he finished, 'the folk in this valley just wouldn't stand a chance against Temple's crew of gunslingers.'

'How many men has Temple got?' McCall asked. 'I owe him too. Never did like being thrown out of a saloon.'

'Near a dozen,' Peckard told him.

'What are you going to do? Take them on single-handed?' Ballard asked.

'Hell, no,' McCall grinned. Then added, 'At least, not until I've had some food. Fighting on an empty stomach ain't good for a man.'

Peckard smiled as he stood up. He put on his hat.

'I better go see about gettin' Quince put under the sod,' he said. 'See you boys later.'

As Peckard stepped out onto the boardwalk, Dicken Hodges burst through the curtained doorway behind the counter. He was followed by a tall, blonde haired woman wearing a pale-blue calico dress and a white apron.

Ballard and McCall rose from their chairs as the woman came across the floor towards them. Beneath the simple dress, which she wore like a silk gown, moved a lithe, sleek body. High, full breasts thrust at the cloth of the bodice, which swept down to a small waist and trim hips. She was brushing a stray lock of hair from her smooth, tanned brow with long, slender fingers.

'I found her,' Hodges said. 'Gents, this is Connie Ward. Owner of the Bonanza.'

'Howdy, ma'am,' Ballard said.

Feeling somehow like a steer that had

wandered into the middle of a wedding party, McCall muttered, 'Ma'am.' *You been spending too much time chasin' cows and not enough chasing girls*, he told himself as he stood there feeling uncomfortable in his worn and dusty clothing.

Connie Ward gave him a quick smile as she said, 'Howdy, yourself, Mr . . . .?'

'Jess McCall, ma'am. And this is Chet Ballard.'

'Welcome to the Bonanza, fellers,' she said. 'Though to look at it now you wouldn't think it was the best eating place in town.'

'I reckon you can blame me for that, ma'am,' McCall said.

Connie smiled. 'Well, if I have to eat my own cooking to get rid of it, I will. But with two big fellers like you to feed I won't need any other customers at all.'

'I'd better wash off some of this dust before I eat,' McCall said. He slapped at his worn shirt and Levis. Dust powdered off at his touch.

'Maybe you'd better,' Connie said. She took him by the arm and led him across the restaurant. 'Sit down, Mr. Ballard,' she called over her shoulder.

Hodges said, 'See you later, I'm gonna get me a drink.'

McCall followed Connie into the well-ordered kitchen. As he passed stoves that held pans of steaming food, his stomach reminded him that he hadn't eaten for a long time.

'There's a pump out back,' Connie said. Then her tone changed. 'Dicken told me what happened. I'm glad you're all right.'

'So am I, ma'am,' McCall said.

Connie smiled again as she handed him a towel and a piece of soap.

'Go get washed, cowboy,' she said.

'Yes, ma'am.'

McCall headed outside into the bright sunlight, saw the pump and began to strip off his shirt.

About five miles to the north of Gunner Creek lay a tall ranch. It was owned by a man called Phil Lansing.

The ranch lay in a good section of land, through which ran the creek that gave the town its name.

The three hands Lansing employed were up in the east section of the spread, doing the last of some late branding. Lansing and his wife had been expecting a quiet day alone. So it had been up until ten minutes ago. Now, their peaceful home had been turned into a place of terror.

While one of the men held her, Mary Lansing watched with horror as two other men beat her husband round the living room of the house. She gave a choking sob as her husband fell. One of the men began to kick Lansing in the stomach.

'*Stop it. You'll kill him, you'll kill him,*' she screamed.

The men took no notice of her. They were all drunk. Very drunk.

They all worked for Wade Temple. Bad enough company when sober. But drunk they were vicious and ugly. Earlier in the day they had ridden out of Gunner Creek, bored by the lack of action in the town. In the pouches of their saddlebags they had carried whisky bottles. As they had ridden they had emptied the bottles. By the time they had reached the Lansing ranch, all three of them were in a dangerous state. They had entered the house by kicking open the door. When Phil Lansing had tried to throw them out, they had attacked him.

The man holding Mary Lansing was called Sam Dugan. At the present time his mind was on something other than concentrating on his companions working over Lansing. The cause of his distraction was Mary Lansing. Even in his drunken state he was able to realize what an attractive woman she was. The feel of her young body against him had aroused his needs for a woman.

'I'm gonna have me a little fun of my own,' he called to his companions. 'Keep him busy.'

Mary Lansing realized his intention when Dugan began to drag her towards the open door of the bedroom.

'No!' she screamed, struggling against Dugan's arms.

Dugan reached the door and shoved her through. Then he slammed the door with a loud crash.

When Dugan finally emerged from the bedroom his two companions were waiting outside the house. Phil Lansing lay motionless on the floor of the living room.

Dugan grinned knowingly at his companions as he mounted up. He led the way and they moved off, heading for the trail that led to Gunner Creek.

4

By the time Ballard and McCall had finished their meal, customers were beginning to drift back into the restaurant. McCall collected his saddlebags and went over to the counter to pay for the meal.

As she took the money, Connie said, 'I hope you boys stay around for a while.'

McCall smiled. 'Might just do that, ma'am.'

Suddenly serious she said, 'Jess, be careful. Temple won't think very kindly of you after what you did.'

'Well, I ain't seen the feller yet myself and I don't cotton to him, so I reckon we're even.'

He turned and threaded his way across the restaurant, oblivious to the stares and whispers from the customers at the tables. As Ballard followed

McCall out the door he turned and raised a hand to Connie Ward and she returned his wave.

Out on the boardwalk McCall paused and said, 'You know where there's a place a body can get some sleep around here?'

'There's a hotel down the street a piece. Got me a room when I rode in this morning,' Ballard said.

Together they headed along the boardwalk, reaching the hotel after couple-of-hundred yards. Like a thousand other trail-town hotels it was in need of paint on its high false front, and the lobby had the same musty smell, with the inevitable potted plants and over-stuffed chairs.

McCall headed for the desk and rang the bell.

'No good that way,' Ballard advised. 'Desk clerk's doesn't hear too well.'

McCall used his fist this time, rattling the shades of the oil-lamps that hung from the ceiling.

From somewhere in the darkness

behind the desk a door opened and a tall, thin man shuffled into the light. His face and hair were practically the same faded shade of white. His big owl-like eyes blinked as he raised them to the level of McCall's face.

'Room?' he asked.

'He catches on fast,' McCall said. He picked up a pen and signed the register.

'How long you figuring to stay?' asked the clerk.

McCall scratched his chin. 'Don't know right off. Better put me down for a week.'

'Pay in advance,' the clerk said. 'That's a dollar a day.'

McCall hauled out his roll of bills and passed across a ten dollar bill.

'Any chance of a bath?' he asked. 'Be extra,' the clerk snapped.

McCall sighed. 'Take it out of the ten.'

'Give a yell when you're ready and I'll have it filled for you.'

'Then you'd better get fillin', slim, 'cause I'm ready now. You give me a yell when it's waitin'.'

The clerk gave a faint smile. 'Yes, sir, right away,' he said.

Ballard led the way up the creaking stairs to the first floor.

'What room you got?' he asked.

'Number nine,' McCall said after he had a look at his key-tag.

'Here you are,' Ballard said. He tapped the door with the toe of his boot.

McCall opened the door and had a quick look round the room. 'Ain't exactly overpowering, is it?' he remarked.

'I'll leave you to get prettied up,' Ballard said.

McCall nodded. 'Okay. See you later on.'

Ballard closed the door as he left.

McCall dumped his saddlebags on the bed and tossed his hat after them. Seating himself on the edge of the bed McCall opened one pouch of the saddlebags and drew out a cloth-wrapped bundle. He unrolled it and exposed a rolled gun rig. The leather of belt and holster, though scarred and worn was supple and oiled. The holster held a .45 caliber Colt's Peacemaker with smooth wood grips. McCall gave a sigh as he withdrew the gun from its sheath. The chamber and frame of the Colt were twisted and gouged. The barrel was offset. McCall eyed the gun sorrowfully. He'd had it a long time, and it had got him out of some tight spots. Then a month ago, in Laramie, a big-mouthed teamster had got into a fight with McCall. Fists had swung, then guns had roared. The end result was that McCall's gun had been hit by a bullet intended for its owner. And the teamster had finished up in the nearest horse trough.

Someone knocked on McCall's door.

'Your bath'll be ready in ten minutes, Mr. McCall,' the clerk's voice said.

'Okay, slim,' he replied.

Stepping into the hot glare of the morning sun Ballard glanced up the street towards the King High debated whether or not to go that way but decided against it for the present. Instead he walked the other way and found himself passing another saloon after about fifty yards. Turning, he pushed through the batwing doors and went in.

Inside it was cool but the tang of stale beer and cigarette smoke hung in the motionless air. Down the left wall ran the bar, with bottle-lined shelves at the back. The remaining floor space was filled with tables and chairs. There were about a dozen men in the place. Ballard headed for the bar.

'How's your beer?' he asked the bartender, a thick-set, heavy jawed individual.

The man ran a pudgy hand across his sweating face. 'Wet,' he said.

'You or the beer?' Ballard inquired.

'The both. You want one?'

Ballard nodded and the bartender bent down behind the counter. When he reappeared he held a large glass of foam-topped beer. Ballard paid for it and carried it to an empty table. He sat down and took a long drink of the amber liquid.

He was enjoying his drink so much he failed to see or hear the three men enter the saloon. The first thing he noticed was the fact that the other customers had fallen completely silent. Ballard finished his drink then placed his glass on the table, at the same time raising his eyes. They stood in front of his table. Three men with the mark of gunslinger written all over them. Though their clothing was just the normal gear worn by most men, it was their gun rigs that set them apart. The tied-down, cutaway holsters, the leather reverently oiled and kept supple. The big heavy Colts, with short barrels and smooth-worn butts.

Here we go, Ballard thought. *Odds on this is something to do with Temple or Rio.*

'Your name Ballard?' one of the men asked. He was a short, heavyset man, with small, close eyes and a greasy mustache that hung over the corners of his hard mouth.

From behind the bar the bartender said, 'Don't start no trouble, Dutch.'

One of the men laughed. 'He wants we should start no trouble, Dutch,' he attacked.

As he spoke he drew his gun and fired. A bottle on the bar exploded in a shower of glass and whisky.

'See, no trouble,' said Dutch. 'We just want this saddle tramp.'

He pushed his hat to the back of his head and grinned at Ballard.

The Texan thought that the only way to even things up a little was to get at them first. He wasted no time on it. Coming to his feet, Ballard grasped the edge of the table and heaved it at the three men. As the table gave him a scant second of time, Ballard used it to reach out and grab the arm of the gunslinger nearest to him. The man gave a yelp of surprise as Ballard yanked him off balance. Then one of Ballard's big fists slammed into the man's stomach, followed by a blow to the jaw that sent him skittering backwards across the saloon.

Dutch and the third man had managed to get clear of the table by now and they moved in on Ballard. Dutch let fly with a swinging left that caught Ballard on the side of the head. Ballard sidestepped to avoid the following punch that Dutch threw and almost stepped into one from the other men. The force of the man's swing brought him close to Ballard. As the man's arm passed the Texan's body, Ballard grabbed it and spun the man round to face him. Then he slammed his fist into the man's face with all his strength. The man spun away with his face streaming blood.

Swinging round to find Dutch, Ballard saw too late the gun in the man's hand. It swept down in a vicious arc and slammed against Ballard's forehead. The Texan was brought to his knees by the blow.

Dimly Ballard made out shapes

before him. Then he felt his arms being grasped and he was hauled to his feet. As his vision cleared he saw Dutch standing before him. Twisting his head he saw it was the two other gunslingers who were holding him. The blow to the head had weakened him so as to make his struggle to get free ineffectual.

'All right, big feller,' Dutch said softly, 'this is a little greeting from a well-wisher. Just to show his feelings for you.'

Ballard tensed himself for what was to come. He saw Dutch draw back his fist, saw it slash forward, felt it slam into his stomach. His breath was forced from his body in a choking rush. His sagging body was hauled upright again. Again Dutch's fist slammed forward. And again and again until Ballard lost count, and interest. The Texan was lost in a world of blackness and pain. After a time he was aware that someone was hitting him in the face. But even that didn't stay with him long. Ballard drifted into emptiness.

When the arms that held him were removed he pitched onto his face. For a few pain-filled seconds he heard voices coming from somewhere far above him. He couldn't make out what they were saying. Then he passed out.

This time completely.

5

Sam Dugan stood in the center of Temple's office. Sweat beaded his face and a thin trickle of blood ran from the corner of his mouth. Behind him stood Rio, his hand close to the butt of his gun.

'Hell, all we did was have a bit of . . . .' Dugan began.

'Shut your mouth,' Temple said savagely. He was standing by the window, gazing down into the street. He was rubbing the back of his left hand where he had hit Dugan.

'You better get out of sight,' Rio said. 'and keep off the streets until this thing is settled.'

Dugan rubbed his bleeding mouth and walked unsteadily out of the office. Rio closed the door behind him and came back across to the window.

'*Idiot*,' Temple said softly.

Rio said, 'Nothing like a woman being raped to set folk off.'

'It's a good thing you got him up here before he told everybody in town.'

Temple moved away from the window and sat down behind his desk.

'Well, we won't be able to stop Lansing telling what happened,' Rio said.

Temple slammed a fist on the top of the desk. 'Damn that stupid animal,' he said.

Rio said, 'I'd better go and see that Dugan keeps out of sight.'

Temple didn't answer so Rio went to the door and let himself out.

As he closed the door, Rio was confronted by Dutch and his two men. One was holding a hand to his bleeding face.

'I see you tangled with him,' Rio said.

Dutch nodded. 'He won't forget us for a while.'

His mouth set in a narrow line, Rio said, 'When I'm finished that bastard will be sorry he ever come looking for us.'

McCall, fresh from his bath and wearing a change of clothing, stepped out of the hotel. He tugged the brim of his hat down to shield his eyes from the glare of the sun. Settling his gun belt firmly on his hip he made off down the boardwalk.

It took him a few minutes before he found what he was looking for. The sign outside the store said: *Joshua Peel, Gunsmith*. McCall went in and up to the oak-topped counter. Behind the counter, on a stool, sat a lean, middle aged man. He was busy working on a double-barreled shotgun. His head came up and his steady eyes gazed up at McCall.

'Howdy,' McCall aid.

'Mornin'.' The gunsmith put down the shotgun and wiped his hands on a rag. 'What can I do for you, mister?'

McCall took out his damaged Colt and laid it on the counter. Peel picked it up and inspected it. Then he shook his head. 'No chance of repair,' he said.

'I reckoned as much,' McCall remarked.

'Think you can sell me another?'

'Will do,' Peel replied. 'What kind you want?'

'Same type. Colt, .45 caliber.'

Peel got of his stool and went to the far end of the counter. He lifted off the top of a glass display-case. McCall saw that it contained a dozen assorted handguns.

'These are all used guns,' Peel said. 'But you'll find some damn good ones amongst em'

McCall took each gun that was handed to him and inspected it with an experienced and critical eye. He hefted and weighed each weapon, trying the action to judge the ease and smooth-ness of the workings. He finally made his choice.

'This feels about right,' he said. 'Good balance, nice action. Could do with the sear filing down a mite.'

'You like a fine trigger?' Peel asked as he took the gun.

'Finer'n a gnat's whisker,' McCall said.

'Won't take but a minute or so,' Peel said. Returning to his stool he brought a box of tools out from beneath the counter. He began to strip the gun to get at the inside mechanism.

McCall watched the gunsmith, fascinated by the man's dexterity. Within ten minutes the job was done and the gun was being reassembled. The completed weapon was handed to McCall.

'Try her now,' Peel said.

McCall hefted the Colt in his big fist. He thumbed back the hammer and touched the trigger. The hammer dropped with a smooth, oiled click. He tried it a few more times, then nodded with satisfaction.

'Much obliged,' he said. 'How much do I owe you?'

When McCall emerged from the gun shop he felt distinctly more at ease than when he had gone in. The now loaded Colt felt good on his right thigh as he began to make his way up the street toward the Sheriff's office.

6

Ernie Peckard paused on the boardwalk outside his office. He was breathing hard and his face was damp with sweat. The old man pushed the office door open, then turned to put an arm around the limp figure leaning against the wall of the jailhouse.

It was Chet Ballard who fell into Peckard's arms as the sheriff pulled him from the wall. The big Texan was still very weak, almost unable to hold himself erect. In fact, Peckard had practically carried the bleeding, semi-conscious man from the saloon where he had found him after the bartender had come and told him what had happened.

Peckard staggered the last few feet into his office and deposited his heavy burden onto the low cot that stood along the left wall. To the right of the door was Peckard's desk. The remainder of the small office was filled by a big pot-bellied stove and a battered filing cabinet. On the wall behind Peckard's desk was a rack that held six rifles and three shotguns. The four cells that took up the rear of the building were all empty. Sunlight filtered in through the two big, barred windows that faced onto the street. Constant exposure to the heat of the reflected sun had long since curled up the edges of the many wanted posters that were tacked up around the walls.

Leaving Ballard for a moment, Peckard closed the door and then crossed over to his desk. From one of the drawers he pulled out a folded pad of white cloth and a jar of ointment. On his way back to the cot he picked up a tin basin and a wooden pail that held clean water. He placed the pail beside the cot and crouched down to inspect Ballard.

The Texan's face was a mass of bruised and cut flesh. Blood streaked his face from one side to the other. The flesh around his eyes was puffy and swollen, his lips split and raw, and there was a two inch gash across his left cheek.

With a sigh Peckard dipped the basin into the water, then tore off a strip of the cloth. Soaking it in the water he began to clean up the mess of Ballard's face.

Ballard suddenly opened his eyes. He tried to sit up. Then he dropped back onto the cot with a deep groan.

'Where am I?' he mumbled through his thick lips.

'In my office,' Peckard said without looking from his task.

Ballard stared at him, winced as Peckard caught a particularly sore spot. 'Man, they really stomped me, huh?'

'Yep,' Peckard nodded. 'Any idea who it was?'

'My vote goes to friend Temple,' Ballard said.

The office door opened just then and Jess McCall came in. He caught sight of

Ballard on the cot as he closed the door.

'What happened?' he asked as he came to stand beside Peckard.

'A little example of our town's hospitality,' Peckard said.

'Looks like I was in the wrong place at the wrong time,' McCall remarked.

Ballard managed a tight grin. 'Never mind. If things go on like they are, you'll be able to do your good deed very soon.'

'Temple?' McCall asked in a voice gone suddenly hard.

Ballard nodded. 'Well, I did come looking for him.'

'You sure do go a funny way about it,' Peckard. said. He stood up, wiping his wet hands on the back of his pants. 'But it ain't likely to get any easier. Like I said before. Temple has too many guns backing him up. You won't get near him.'

Ballard sat up slowly. 'Maybe,' he said. He ran his hands through his hair. 'The warning those three were handing out was clear enough. Get out before you buck something you can't handle.'

'I reckon it's 'bout time somebody gave Mr. Temple a warning all his own,' McCall said abruptly. 'Ain't there anything we can do, Sheriff.'

'I'm one old man, boy,' Peckard said. 'And I ain't ashamed to say I'm *too* old to go up against Temple and his crew alone.'

'Ain't you got deputies?' McCall asked.

Peckard gave a dry laugh. 'Never had much need for 'em until lately. Last one I had quit when Temple's men got a little rough.'

'You still got his badge?' McCall inquired casually.

Peckard nodded, asked, 'Why?'

'Maybe you got yourself someone to wear it.'

'*You?* For God's sake why?' Peckard exclaimed. 'Look, boy, you got no cause to do anything for this town. Only a while back they stood by and watched while you were nearly gunned down. If

57

it hadn't been for Ballard you'd be a dead man now.'

McCall scratched the back of his head. 'I know all that, Sheriff, but I reckon I'm the kind of feller who don't like to see folk being put on. Maybe if I was in their place I'd be just as scared as they are.'

Peckard shock his head slowly. 'Maybe I know what you're trying to say, boy, but do you know what you're getting into?'

'Reckon so,' McCall said. 'Anyhow, it'll be interestin'.'

Peckard looked doubtful. 'That still only makes two of us against the whole of Temple's crew, boy.'

The cot creaked as Ballard got unsteadily to his feet.

'Three,' he said.

Peckard glanced at him. 'You too? Either they hit you too hard or all those stories about Texans being fighting mad are true.'

Ballard smiled. 'It's like this, Sheriff. I've been after Temple and Rio for a long time. Had a lot of fool ideas about how to get even with them. But since I've been in town I've done some thinking. See, I've worn a badge before, and it makes a man aware of the law. I reckon if I put on a star now, I'll be able to see that Temple gets what he's earned the right way. Feel better about it, too.'

Peckard crossed to his desk and opened a top drawer. He took out two tarnished badges.

'They need polishing a mite,' he said in a shaky voice. Then he cleared his throat, and a gleam came into his old eyes. 'By hell, we'll give Mr. Temple a good shake, I reckon. Raise your right hands.'

As McCall pinned on his badge, then raised his hand, he realized what he *was* doing. And he also got to asking himself *why* he was doing it. *Hell*, he thought, *I only stopped over to have a damn game of cards*. Now I'm going to start to clean the place up. He made a silent promise to himself that the next time he

7

The rest of the day dragged by without further incidents. On the surface everything looked calm. But beneath the forced air of peace and quiet lay a dark, brooding cloud that hinted of trouble to come in the near future.

Jess McCall and Chet Ballard went about the routine duties as Peckard's deputies. Though the town appeared to be normal, as they made the rounds, the Texans could sense the atmosphere of hostility that hung over it like a thunder cloud. Though there were a few people on the boardwalks it was no effort for Ballard or McCall to pick out Temple's gunslingers.

The Temple crew must have had orders to keep out of trouble for the time being. Though they gave the two deputies the impression that a gunfight was what they wanted they hung back with obvious reluctance.

It hadn't taken long for the news to reach the ears of Wade Temple that Peckard had taken on the two Texans as deputies. The news had taken Temple by surprise. This was something unexpected. If Peckard was taking on deputies it meant that he was thinking about making a fight for his town. And men like Ernie Peckard who fought for a cause were sometimes hard to stop. So Temple had some thinking to do. His first demand was that his men would make no attempt at starting anything until Temple himself gave the word.

Rio hadn't liked it.

'Look,' he said, as he came into Temple's office, 'why don't we go and take them straight off. Before they get properly organized. If we leave it too long they might talk some of the townsmen into a fighting mood.'

'Rio, listen up,' Temple said. 'You had your chance and you messed it up. If I'd had it my way, Ballard would be out of our way for good. But you had to start thinking and have him roughed up. All you did was to make him more determined to get at *us*.'

Rio didn't like being talked to in that way and his narrow face hardened, his eyes turned cold and black. A muscle in his jaw jerked as he fought to suppress the violent emotions that tried to rip their way from his body.

'So what *do* we do?' he asked finally, his voice almost a whisper.

Temple, his eyes on the hand that lingered near Rio's gun butt, said, 'We wait until I decide what to do. Tell the men to keep away from Peckard and his deputies. Right away. And make sure that bastard, Dugan, keeps out of sight.'

★   ★   ★

The heat of the day soon turned to a sharp chill as night came on.

While Ballard looked after the office, Ernie Peckard and McCall took the job of night-watch. It was an uneventful, but cold one. At three o' clock the following morning Ballard and McCall went to their hotel rooms for some sleep. Peckard stayed on at the jail, bunking down on the cot.

By mid-morning the town was baking under a hot sun. Ernie Peckard and his new deputies were coming out of the Bonanza Restaurant, after a late breakfast, when a fair sized piece of hell went and exploded right in the center of main street.

It came in the form of Phil Lansing, driving a racing buckboard up from the north end of town. It hurtled along the middle of the wide street in a thud of horses' hooves and a swirling cloud of dust, scattering men and horses that got in its way.

Peckard suddenly said, 'God, it's Phil Lansing'

He ran forward, off the boardwalk and into the street, waving his arms, shouting.

The driver of the buckboard must

have seen the sheriff for he suddenly hauled in the reins, bringing the horses to a plunging halt.

Peckard ran to the buckboard. McCall was close behind him.

'Phil, what's happened?' Peckard asked. Then he saw the condition of Lansing's face.

Lansing didn't answer as he threw himself from the seat and went to the rear of the buckboard.

'Not Mary'?' Peckard said, his voice taut.

Mary Lansing lay on the wooden floor of the buckboard, covered by thick blankets. Her face was bruised, and her eyes were wide and staring, completely unseeing.

Peckard grasped Lansing by the shoulders and turned him round.

'Phil, what happened? Who did this to you and Mary'?'

Lansing lifted his head. His face was one mass of ugly, bruised and cut flesh. 'Sam Dugan,' he said flatly, his voice without emotion. '*Sam Dugan.*'

'One of Temple's crew?' McCall asked.

'Yeah,' Peckard replied.

A few onlookers had crowded round and one of them stepped up to Peckard. 'Sheriff, over there,' he said, indicating something with his arm.

'What is it?' Ballard asked.

Peckard nodded across the street to where three men were standing at the edge of the boardwalk.

'Know 'em?' McCall asked.

Peckard nodded. 'Big feller in front is Sam Dugan,' he said.

At the sound of Dugan's name being spoken Phil Lansing jerked his head round. He saw the three men on the far boardwalk. A cry of anger came from his throat as he threw himself towards the buckboard. His outstretched hands clawed beneath the buckboard's seat, and came out grasping a heavy double-barreled shotgun.

Peckard saw the rancher's intention and he stepped in front of him. 'Phil, don't,' he said. 'Let me handle it.'

But Lansing paid no attention to the lawman. It was as if he couldn't see anything except the three gunslingers across the street.

'*Dugan, I'm going to kill you!*' Lansing's voice was high with emotion. He pushed past Peckard hard, heading for the end of the buckboard.

Peckard swung after him and grabbed Lansing's arm. For a moment they struggled. Then Lansing swung the butt of the shotgun into Peckard's stomach. The old man fell to his knees with a groan.

'*Hey!*' McCall yelled.

Lansing cleared the end of the buckboard and headed across the street, swinging up the shotgun.

Dugan and his companions saw the approaching rancher and realized he meant business. They split their group and went for their guns.

As Lansing began to raise his shotgun, McCall, who had followed him out, ran at the rancher. He slammed his full weight into Lansing.

67

The two of them hit the ground with a hard slam. Lansing's finger jerked the shotgun's triggers and both barrels fired. The blast of shot howled into the air.

Before the boom of the shotgun had faded there came the heavy roar of handguns. Slugs kicked up spurts of dirt around McCall and Phil Lansing. McCall shoved Lansing away from him as he pushed to his feet. As his hand dropped to his holster, McCall felt a slug burn a line across the side of his neck. Then McCall swung up his Colt, thumbed back the hammer and touched the trigger. He felt the gun buck in his palm as it fired, saw one of the men on the boardwalk twist sideways and plunge forward onto the street.

Behind McCall, Ballard was exchanging shots with Dugan. Unlike his opponent Ballard was forcing himself to stay calm. Without a second of haste the Texan drew a bead on Dugan and squeezed the trigger twice. Dugan uttered a scream of terror as Ballard's slugs tore into him. He was swept back across the board-walk, hitting the wall behind him. He hung there for a brief moment his eyes fixed on the spurting streams of bright blood that pumped out of the holes in his chest. Then he slowly toppled to the boardwalk, his head striking hard against the planking.

In the momentary lull that followed, the surviving gunman did the wisest thing of his life. He threw aside his gun and raised his arms above his head, and began shouting, '*I quit. Don't shoot!*'

McCall glanced behind him. Ernie Peckard was leaning up against the side of the buckboard and Ballard was moving across the street toward the surrendered gunslinger. Holstering his gun McCall helped Lansing to his feet. The rancher ran a hand across his battered face.

'Sorry,' he mumbled faintly.

McCall rubbed the spot on his neck where the slug had burned him.

'Don't let it worry you none,' he said

As McCall and Lansing reached the buckboard, Ballard joined them with his prisoner. Peckard nodded in the direction of the two bodies.

'Both dead,' Ballard informed him.

'You all right, Sheriff?' McCall asked.

'I'll live,' Peckard said. 'Teach me not to get in the way of a man's gun butt.'

Lansing cleared his throat uncomfortably. He raised his eyes to meet Peckard's unflinching gaze. His swollen lips moved slowly. 'I . . . I . . . don't know how to apologize, Ernie,' he said.

Peckard chuckled gently. 'Hell, Phil,' he said, 'if I thought you'd really meant that punch, I'd have put a slug in your leg.'

'You want this in jail?' Ballard asked, indicating his sullen prisoner.

'Give him the best cell we got,' said Peckard. To the gunman he snapped, 'You've just left Temple's payroll, Tanner.'

Tanner gave a crooked grin. 'Listen, old man, you won't have me in that place long enough to lock the door. You

70

carved your own headstone when you tangled with us.'

'Hey, this feller scares me,' McCall said soberly.

Ballard gave Tanner a not too gentle push towards the jail. 'Move out, mister.'

'Somebody help Phil and Mary over to Doc Burkett's office. He should be back from Joe Haskell's place by now.' Peckard turned to the gathered crowd as he spoke.

Two men stepped forward. One helped Phil Lansing onto the front seat of the buckboard. The other climbed in the back with Mary Lansing. Phil Lansing sat still and erect as the buckboard moved off up the street towards the end of town where Gunner Creek's doctor had his office.

A familiar figure appeared in front of McCall. It was Dicken Hodges. He reeked of whisky and carried a bottle in each hand.

'Hey, boy,' he said loudly, 'you sure are one big hell raiser. Wherever you go you stir up trouble.' He grinned up at McCall. Then he turned to Peckard. 'Hey, Ernie,' he shouted, 'you done got you a couple of dandy deputies.'

Peckard nodded. 'Seems so, Dicken. Say, do something for me, huh. Go tell Jerry Sol there are two customers for him.'

Swinging his whisky bottles Hodges made off up the street.

'Who is Jerry Sol?' McCall asked, already guessing the answer.

'*Undertaker*,' Peckard replied. Then he said, 'Let's go see how our one-and-only prisoner is doing.'

8

Temple was in his office, going through his accounts when the door burst open and Dutch Canfield came in.

'What the hell do you want?' Temple snapped. He was in a touchy mood. He'd had very little sleep the previous night, due to the fact that the problems of Peckard, his two deputies and now Dugan, were constantly at the forefront of his thoughts. 'Well?' he asked again.

'Trouble,' Dutch said. 'Dugan, Tanner, and Wylie have gone out.'

'*What!*' Temple exploded, his anger bursting free. 'I told them to keep out of circulation until I got everything sorted out about Lansing.'

'Yeah, I know,' Dutch said. 'But Dugan don't like to be shoved around too much. He said he wasn't going to stay inside for you or anybody. Not while he has anything to say about it.'

'That ignorant bastard could make big trouble,' Temple said. 'Get Rio up here. Fast!'

As Dutch turned towards the door there came a sudden outburst of gunfire from the direction of the street. Temple ran to the window, pushed it open and leaned out. Dutch joined him. They were in time to see the end of the fight. Temple watched in bitter silence as Chet Ballard escorted Vic Tanner over to the jail. He saw Ernie Peckard and Jess McCall standing beside a buckboard, saw them turn towards the jail as the buckboard moved off.

'Seems like that old law dog ain't as useless as we been imagining,' Dutch remarked.

Temple wasn't impressed by the observation. 'Damn that stupid old fool. Does he think he can make a stand against us?'

'He's made a good start,' Dutch said.

'Whose side are you on?' Temple

asked, his face darkened by an angry scowl.

Dutch pulled his head back into the office. He waited until Temple had closed the window.

'What now?' he asked.

Temple picked up his hat and strode to the door.

'Bring a couple of the men. And find Rio. We're going to pay a visit to the sheriff's office. It's about time I had a talk with the law of this town. Someone seems to have the wrong impression as to which hand holds the whip around here.'

It was only a few minutes later that Temple, along with Rio, Dutch Canfield, and two more of his hired guns, left the King High and made their way up the street towards the town jail.

Rio walked alongside of Temple. The expression of cynical amusement on Rio's face annoyed Temple. He had the feeling that Rio was only along for the ride. Just lately he had been pushing a little too hard. He never passed up an opportunity to make one of his biting comments at Temple. The man seemed to take delight in taking sharp jabs at Temple's pride. Temple put it down to the fact that Rio was getting tired of the set-up here in Gunner Creek. Maybe he was thinking of moving on.

If he was, Temple thought, *there was a way it could be arranged.*

Temple pushed the thoughts to the back of his mind as he found himself standing before the jail. He glanced over his shoulder. Dutch stood a few feet to one side with his two men. Rio was on Temple's left, still with a cold glimmer of a smile on his face. Temple's mouth stiffened for a moment. Then he looked away and faced the jail.

'Peckard,' he called, 'come out here. I want to talk to you.'

The jail door opened before Temple had finished speaking.

Ernie Peckard came out and walked to the edge of the boardwalk. He was followed by Jess McCall and Chet

Ballard. Both of the Texans carried rifles.

For a moment Temple forgot his reason for coming as he gazed up at Chet Ballard.

'Nice day, gents,' Ballard said pleasantly. But he was looking at Temple as he spoke, and his words brought a sudden chill that made Temple's flesh creep.

9

Ballard had Tanner locked in one of the cells by the time McCall and Peckard got back to the jail.

'Man, what a day,' McCall said as he shut the door.

Ballard was sitting on the edge of the desk thumbing shells into a rifle. He glanced up and said, 'You wanted the job.'

'Yeah, I know.' McCall indicated the rifle. 'You expecting more?'

'I don't think Temple is going to let this go unheeded.'

'He's right,' Peckard said. 'If we can get away with a thing like this, it's going to show the folks in town that Temple isn't untouchable. *They* might get the notion to start something, too.'

McCall got himself a rifle and began to load it.

For a few minutes the office was

silent, save for the sound of guns being checked and loaded. Each man looked to his weapon with the almost religious reverence of men who know that their lives depend on the perfect working of their chosen gun.

From outside came the sound of Wade Temple's voice.

Peckard made for the door. As he began to open it he spoke over his shoulder.

'Keep your eyes open. Don't trust a single one of Temple's crew.'

The Texans were close behind Peckard as he stepped out of the office. The sheriff walked to the edge of the boardwalk and stopped. McCall and Ballard flanked him, their rifles held relaxed but ready to be swung into use.

When Ballard broke the premature silence that hung over the two groups Peckard was swift to take notice of the effects that his words produced.

Temple's reaction was plain to see. Noticeable too was the hard smile on Rio's face. He seemed to be totally indifferent to the fact that he was facing a man who had witnessed him commit murder.

'You want to see me?' Peckard asked sharply, making the most of Temple's momentary confusion.

Temple turned his gaze on Peckard. He drove back the eddying waves of fear that were threatening to break his composure. With a firmness come of long practice he forced himself speak steadily.

'What's this game you're playing, Peckard? Two of my men dead and another in jail. And Quince shot yesterday, by a saddle tramp now your deputy.'

McCall stepped up to the edge of the boardwalk. His face was hard as he said, 'I'd watch that loose mouth, mister. Could get you in a lot of trouble.'

Peckard said, 'Your man, Tanner, is in jail because he drew down on me and my deputies. Dugan and Wylie are dead because they tried the same thing, only they chose the hard way out. Quince, well he got what he'd been working towards for a while.'

Temple's eyes narrowed and his face darkened. 'How long do you expect to keep Tanner locked up?' he demanded.

'As long as it takes to get the circuit judge to come and try him.'

At this Temple gave a grunt of annoyance. 'Now look, Peckard,' he snapped, 'I don't think you realize what you're doing.'

Peckard smiled tiredly as he said: 'Temple, I know what I'm doing. It's something that should have been done a long time ago. And it's the matter of cleaning this town of you and your crew of no-good, bullying scum. Now, I'm an old man, but as long as I wear this star I'm the law. And from now on I'm going to do everything I can to get rid of you, Temple, any way I can.'

Rio suddenly stepped up to the boardwalk, his face devoid of any expression.

'*Old man*, why don't you put away

the badge and join the rest of the old timers in the sun.' His voice was low and goading.

Out of the corner of his eye McCall saw Peckard stiffen. He saw the sheriff's hand moving toward his gun butt. He realized that this was what Rio wanted Peckard to do. Go for his gun and be dropped by Rio, who would then claim self-defense. McCall didn't hesitate. He took one step forward, off the boardwalk and onto the street. As he came alongside of Rio the Texan swung his rifle in a short, swift arc. The hard barrel came down on Rio's gun hand with a sharp crack. Rio's lips drew back in a grimace of pain and his head swung round.

'Careless of me,' McCall said apologetically.

Rio made a sound deep in his throat. His face showed every last vestige of hate he carried. *If looks could kill,* McCall thought at that moment, *I would be one dead Texican boy.*

Peckard broke the silence then.

'Temple, if any of your boys even look at me wrong, I'll put them away.'

Temple seemed lost for words. 'You won't be able to hide behind that badge for long, Peckard,' he blustered.

He turned and walked away, followed by his crew. Only Rio remained. He stood for a moment, nursing his hand.

'This isn't over,' he said.

McCall nodded. 'Damn right it isn't.'

Rio looked as if he might still be going to go for his gun, but he thought better of it and withdrew.

McCall took off his hat and wiped his face on his sleeve.

'Close enough there to shave,' he said.

'Too close,' Ballard agreed. 'Next time won't finish so quietly.'

Peckard nudged McCall's arm 'Thanks for getting Rio off my back.'

McCall grinned. 'Only did it 'cause it's your turn to buy the coffee.'

'Okay,' Peckard said, 'let's go before I change my mind.'

10

As Wade Temple strode back to the King High after his meeting with Ernie Peckard he felt flickering's of fear. His mind was in a turmoil as he strove to find a solution to his problems.

He realized that Peckard was in complete earnest about getting tough. And having those deputies was in Peckard's favor. Ballard would stick with the job till he saw that Temple was either finished or dead. The other one, McCall, was one of those Texans who loved a fight, and loved it more if it was for a cause. Temple swore silently as he reviewed the incident with the Lansings. The attack itself was bad enough. But what Temple was perturbed about was the way that Peckard and his deputies had taken on three of his crew and come out of it unharmed.

Temple entered the saloon and

straightaway went up to his office. To be alone was what he wanted just now. He found his hands were trembling as he went over to the cabinet where he kept his drink and poured himself a large shot of whisky.

Sitting behind his desk Temple took a long swallow from his glass. The whisky coursed down his throat, making his eyes narrow as it burned a searing path through his body. This time though the effect was not the usual one that whisky had on him. Instead of making him feel secure and optimistic, the whisky became a damper, lowering his morale and leaving a bitter tang in his mouth. With a sudden outburst of frustration Temple hurled the glass across the room. It shattered against the far wall and the whisky stained the wallpaper, running down to the carpet in long glistening streaks.

Temple pushed to his feet and strode over to the window. He gazed down on a near-deserted street.

Damn this town, he thought savagely.

He began to realize just how much he really hated Gunner Creek. His grip on the town had become so tight that he was slowly strangling it. The place was becoming a tomb, a dead town filled with frightened, dumb sheep. He shouted, they jumped. He demanded something, they gave it without a murmur.

Temple spun away from the window and began to pace back and forth across the carpeted floor.

To Temple the situation was worrying. He was a man who liked all things to go in his favor. If things began to move along the wrong road, Temple would not, like most men, make a fight. His way was to take what could be salvaged and go before he was pushed against a wall and forced to fight to keep his own. That was not Wade Temple's way. Because if one got involved in a fight, there was only one outcome. One side would emerge victorious, the other would carry the burden of defeat. And defeat could mean death to the loser.

In a single word lay the point to which all Temple's fears and thoughts were channeled. Wade Temple was a men who loathed the thought of death with a deep-rooted revulsion. His life was the most precious thing he had and he intended to keep it for a long time. Therefore, he was ready to do anything to protect it. He would stop at nothing if it enabled him to go on existing. And here was the reason for Temple' current concerns. He was now realizing the situation that was developing looked like the start of something liable to spread. Let the town see the effect of Peckard and his deputies, and they too might get the courage to fight for their freedom. Whatever the size of his crew, Temple knew it would be the finish of him in Gunner Creek. When that time came, Wade Temple would not be around to feel the fury of a town's revenge. He had no desire to end up dangling from the end of a rope. Before that time came he would be long gone from this place.

His decision made, Temple swung into feverish action.

With his mind made up settled, he became his calm self again as he crossed his office and opened the door. He stepped across the corridor to the railing that edged it. He looked down into the saloon below, to where Rio sat at a table. With Rio was Dutch Canfield. Over at the bar were the two gunslingers who were with Dutch constantly, Hal Weston and Burt Nels.

As he stared down at Rio's slim back, Temple was reminded of the man's actions earlier. Temple couldn't make any sense out of Rio's behavior. He couldn't decide whether Rio's move had been a desire to help, or just to hinder matters. Of late Rio had been a definite thorn in Temple's side. So Temple made another decision. This one concerned Rio. With cold, deliberate intent Temple made the disposal of Rio one of the things to be done before he left Gunner Creek. And, Temple thought, he would do it himself. Now he leaned over the railing and called, 'Dutch, come up to the office. Something I want to see you about.'

Dutch glanced up at Temple, then across at Rio. The gunslinger ignored him. Dutch got up and headed for the stairs. Temple waited a few seconds then turned and went back into his office.

They were in the Bonanza restaurant. Ernie Peckard placed his empty cup on the table and leaned back in his chair. He gazed at the faces of Ballard and McCall for a few moments. Then he gave a slow smile.

'Hells fire, I never seen Temple as rattled as he was today,' he said.

McCall nodded. 'He don't like being pushed, that's his trouble. He wants to be to be top of the heap all the time.'

'I don't want to be a sour face,' said Ballard, 'but Temple ain't the sort to be told what he can't do or have. We might have had a small victory today, but I wouldn't count on it lasting too long. With a feller like Wade Temple it's impossible to determine what he'll do next.'

Peckard said, 'I agree with you. That's what makes this mess hard to figure. Not knowing what's going to happen.'

'Well why not have some more coffee while you're waiting,' said Connie Ward. She had come up to the table without them hearing. In her hand she held a large coffee-pot.

'That's for me,' McCall said.

Connie filled his cup, then Ballard's. Peckard declined more as he stood up.

'I'll make tracks back to the jail and see how our boarder is,' he said. 'You boys finish your coffee then join me. Connie.'

Peckard put on his hat and left the restaurant.

McCall leaned back in his chair and gave a contented sigh. He saw Connie watching him and grinned.

'Where did you learn to make coffee

like that?' he asked.

'Old family secret,' Connie said. She gazed round the empty restaurant and shook her head. 'Maybe I'm losing my touch. Place is usually full about this time.'

'Blame us for that,' Ballard said. 'Since that fracas with Temple's men the town's been very quiet. I reckon we must have upset some folk.'

'It'll do them good,' Connie said sharply. 'It's about time the people in this town realized that Wade Temple has had his way for too long. It makes me mad when two complete strangers have to help because a bunch of people are too frightened to fight for their own town.'

McCall said, 'That was some speech. Hey, you should do that more often, Connie, you look good when you're angry.'

'Can't you ever be serious, Jess?'

'Not for long,' McCall admitted. 'Only when I'm playing poker or kissing a pretty girl.'

'If your kissing gets the same results as your poker, you're going to be buried laughing your head off,' Ballard said.

'You two are just making fun of me,' Connie said.

McCall suddenly asked, 'When did it rain here last?'

'Six, seven months ago. Why?'

McCall pointed out of the window. Off to the north they saw dark angry clouds rolling towards the town.

'They look like storm clouds,' Ballard remarked.

'Maybe a good storm is what we want,' said Connie. 'Might cool off some of the hot tempered folk around here.'

Ballard said, 'We better get back on the job, Jess.'

'Okay,' McCall replied. He finished off his coffee and rose from his chair.

'Watch out for yourselves,' Connie called as the Texans headed for the door.

'Sure thing,' McCall said.

Out on the boardwalk they stopped

and took in the completely deserted street. No horses stood at the hitch rails. The place looked as though it had been deserted by people for a long time. It was quiet. Too quiet. An ominous, deadly silence that put Ballard and McCall on edge.

Dropping his hand to the butt of his Colt McCall loosened it in its holster.

'Maybe I'm just a mite nervous,' he said, 'but I get the feeling that we're sitting targets for anyone who cares to try.'

Ballard's face was turned away from the street. He said, 'Hang on to that feeling, Jess. There are around half-a-dozen rifles kind of aimed this way right now.'

As he spoke there came the sharp, spiteful crack of a rifle. The slug tore into the boardwalk at Ballard's feet. Then a number of guns added their deadly sound to the echo of the first.

11

When Dutch Canfield entered the office Temple was waiting with a couple of glasses of whisky.

'Close the door, Dutch,' Temple said.

Dutch shut the door, then crossed the office and took the glass that Temple offered him.

'Sit down,' Temple said.

Dutch sat down as Temple cleared his throat, then said, 'Dutch, I'm getting out of here. Going a long way. I'd like you along. And I can make it worth your while.'

Dutch drained his glass and wiped the ends of his mustache with the back of his hand.

'Sounds promising,' Dutch said. His eyes were fixed intently on Temple. 'Who else you want to come along?' he asked.

'I was thinking about Nels and

Weston. You think they'll come? It means running out on the rest of the crew.'

'Hell,' Dutch laughed, 'who gives a damn about them. If they get the wrong end of the stick it don't mean a thing to me. That's what Burt and Hal will tell you, too. Why, if they got a chance to make a buck they'd gun each other.'

Temple smiled. He took Dutch's glass and refilled it. Then he perched himself on the edge of his desk.

'If we work this right we can live high, Dutch. The way things are going we haven't any future here in Gunner Creek.'

'So we go while we still can, huh?' Dutch finished.

'Precisely.'

Dutch got up from his chair and crossed to the window. He gazed out for a while, then turned, rubbing his jaw.

'How do we do our vanishing trick without everybody noticing? I don't reckon anyone's just going to let us go without trying to stop us.'

'I been thinking on that,' Temple said. 'If there was a gunfight going on, I don't think anyone would notice us riding out. And if we took off across the valley from behind the saloon, the chances of being spotted would be lessened even more.'

'It'd work, alright,' Dutch said. 'But how about the fight?'

Temple gave a quick smile. 'Easy enough, Dutch. Since those two deputies gunned down Dugan the rest of the crew have been itching to get at them. The only thing stopping them is my say so. If I let them loose, I'll guarantee all hell will break free.'

Dutch asked, 'When do we start?'

'Right now,' Temple said. 'When you get downstairs you can tell the men that Ballard and McCall are all their very own. Peckard, too, if they want him. Then take Nels and get four good mounts from the livery stable. You'd better get food and water too. When it's all ready, get round to the rear door of the saloon and pick up Weston and me.'

'Okay,' Dutch said. 'You want Hal up here?'

'Yes. He can give me a hand with the money.'

As soon as Dutch had left the office Temple headed for the iron safe that stood behind his desk. Swiftly he worked the combination and swung open the heavy door. The interior of the safe was stacked with neat piles of banknotes. Almost two-hundred thousand dollars. The wealth of Gunner Creek. But Temple had no time to dwell on the methods he had used to get it at the moment. He rose and turned to his desk. From a bottom drawer he took two sets of saddlebags. Returning to the safe he began to pack the money into the pouches. When the last bundle of notes had been put away he strapped up the saddlebags and lifted them onto the desk.

A sudden knock on the door sent him clawing for his gun. He checked himself and ran his hands through his hair. Temple found he was sweating heavily.

'Yes?' he asked, trying to sound calm.

'It's Weston,' came the reply.

'Come on in.' Weston came in and closed the door. He waved an arm in the direction of the window.

'You seen the sky?' he asked.

Temple looked out of the window, up at the dark clouds that were blotting out the normal blue of the sky.

'Looks like we may be going to have some rain. I hope so. Be in our favor if it does. Tracks soon get washed away in a rainstorm. It would help us a lot.'

'Dutch gave the crew your orders. They sure seem anxious to get at them Texans.'

'Good. It looks like we're going to make our move without anyone noticing.'

Weston indicated the saddlebags on the desk. 'Those what you want me to take down to Dutch?'

Temple nodded. He handed one of the strapped up sets to Weston.

'Get yourself down the rear stairs and wait for Dutch.'

'What about you?' Weston asked.

Temple smiled. 'I'll be down as soon as I get a matter settled. We wait for the shooting to start, then we ride.'

Weston nodded. He slung the saddle-bags over his shoulder and opened the office door. As he went out a shadow fell across the floor from out in the corridor. Temple glanced up and saw Rio standing there, an odd expression on his lean face.

'I want to see you,' Rio said. He came into the office and shut the door with a crash.

Temple forced himself to be calm as he faced Rio.

'Sure, Rio. What is it?'

'I'll tell you,' Rio said. 'I'm wondering what the hell is going on around here. I hear you let the crew loose on Peckard and his deputies.'

'That's right, Rio. Since you failed to get rid of Ballard I'm doing it my way.'

Temple went across to the cabinet

99

and poured two fresh glasses of whisky. He handed one to Rio. The gunman took it and stood watching Temple closely.

'What are you trying to pull, Wade?' he asked suddenly.

For a moment Temple had to fight back a rising tide of panic. He took a long drink from his glass and allowed the whisky to settle the churning in his stomach.

'I don't know what you mean, Rio,' he said calmly.

Rio leaned against the edge of Temple's desk. His lean face held an expression of contempt. He shook his head slowly, saying: 'You can't fool me. You're pulling some stunt. And you've got Dutch, Nels, and Weston in on it. What is it? Are you lighting out?'

Temple didn't answer the questions. Because at that moment the thing he'd been hoping, almost praying for, happened. The explosive roar of many guns. It seemed that his plan was working. Sooner than he'd expected.

But at the most opportune moment.

At the sound of the gunfire Rio's head jerked round towards the window. Temple used this moment to spring his trap. His right hand, moist with sweat, swept down for his gun. His clawing fingers curled around the butt and the .44 came up smoothly, the hammer going back with an oiled click.

Rio's head swung back at the sound. His mouth narrowed as he saw the black muzzle aimed at him.

'*Double-crossing . . .* ' Then his own hand released the whisky glass and streaked down to his holster.

Wade Temple's finger tightened on the trigger he was thinking, *He's still going to beat me! He's going to fire first!*

Then the .44 bucked and roared. Flame lanced from the muzzle and Rio was slammed backwards by the impact of the slug. Temple fired again. Rio slid across the top of the desk, then fell out of sight behind it, overturning the chair as he dropped to the floor.

Temple stood motionless for a moment. Then he heaved a great sigh and ran his hand across his eyes. He dropped his gun back in its holster. He picked up the remaining pair of saddlebags, put on his hat, and went out of the office. He closed the door behind him, then made his way along the corridor to the door that led to the rear stairs.

He made his way swiftly to the bottom to where Dutch, Nels, and Weston were waiting on fresh mounts. Temple secured the saddlebags on the fourth horse, then mounted up.

'Let's ride,' he said.

The four moved out at a gallop, heading for the empty flats that lay beyond town, and the range of hills that lay in the distance.

Not one of them was aware that they had been observed as they rode off: by old Dicken Hodges, who had been sleeping off the effects of a big bottle-party. The old man had been awakened by the sound of their departure. Hodges stood watching the four riders as they headed across the wide flats. Then he turned and stood listening to the rattle of gunfire from the other side of the saloon.

Before the splinters of wood ripped up by the first volley of shots had reached the boardwalk again, McCall had given Ballard a shove.

'Head for home,' he yelled.

Ballard took the advice and broke into a run, McCall close behind. They kept close up to the walls of the buildings, hoping to get some sort of cover from the shadows that lay there. Howling slugs followed their progress as they ran almost on all fours. Ballard felt a slug tug at the sleeve of his shirt.

Then McCall lost his footing and fell. He came to his feet in time to see three men running out of an alley across the street. The three had guns in their hands, and they were using them.

'*Chet, watch it!*' McCall yelled.

Ballard swung around and saw the three.

As McCall drew his Colt he felt a slug tear into his left arm. He thumbed back the Colt's hammer and let go a shot. Beside him, Ballard had added his own Colt. Between them the Texans set up a hail of lead that put the three gunslingers down before they were halfway across the street.

Further down the street men came out of the King High. McCall saw them. He prodded Ballard and indicated the men.

'Time to retreat,' Ballard said.

They reached the jail with lead snapping viciously around them. As they came up to the door it swung open and a rifle poked out and began to spit flame and smoke from its muzzle. Keeping low the Texans went in fast. They heard the door slam shut with a heavy crash.

Ernie Peckard, rifle in his hand, leaned against the wall beside the door. He had a smile on his face when he said, 'When I was a young'un we ran a lot faster than that when somebody shot at us.'

McCall was ripping away his blood-soaked sleeve.

'I ain't exactly built for runnin'. Sooner have me a good horse any day.'

Outside the firing had died away. For a while it seemed that they were to have a brief respite.

Ballard set himself the job of loading the guns while Peckard cleaned up McCall's arm. The bullet had only left a flesh wound.

'Well,' McCall said, 'it seems you were right about not knowing what to expect from Temple.'

'I knew he'd make some move,' Peckard said. 'But this is one I didn't expect.'

Abruptly the light began to fade and darken. Beyond the office windows the empty street took on the desolate look of a ghost town. The sky above Gunner Creek was black from the storm clouds that had been moving that way most of the morning.

The first raindrops fell and were

sucked away by the parched, dry earth. But in the next few seconds the full power of the storm unleashed itself on the town. The rain came in solid, blinding sheets. Bouncing and drumming off the rooftops and gathering in ever widening pools in the streets and alleys.

'Does it always rain like this around here?' McCall asked.

Peckard glanced up from the strip of cloth he was wrapping round McCall's arm.

'Hell, no,' he said, 'this is nothing but a heavy dew.' McCall grinned and Ballard gave a deep chuckle. The steady hiss of the rain was suddenly shattered by the unmistakable boom of rifle fire.

'I thought they'd quit for a while,' McCall remarked.

Ballard went across to one of the windows and peered through the rain-streaked glass.

'*Hey!*' he said. 'Look here.'

Peckard and McCall joined him at the window and stared out of the water

— rippled glass.

Even in the dim light and the slashing rain, the lean figure of Dicken Hodges was easily identified. The ex-buffalo hunter was running across the street at a low crouch. Beyond him, coming from the King High were the moving shapes of armed men.

'What the hell is that old coot trying to do,' Peckard exploded. 'If he wants to commit suicide he's going the right way.'

Ballard grabbed up a couple of rifles and tossed one to McCall. He knocked the door latch up and swung the door open. Rain swept into the office as Ballard stepped out onto the board-walk, bringing up his rifle. McCall was close behind him. Glass shattered as Peckard shoved his rifle butt through the window. Empty brass shell cases began to litter the boardwalk as the three set up a rapid withering fire.

'Head it up, old timer,' McCall yelled as he substituted his Colt for his empty rifle.

'Hell's fire, I ain't a hoss,' Hodges grumbled as he swung up onto the boardwalk and into the jail.

With Hodges inside, Ballard and McCall backed swiftly through the door. Peckard kicked it shut. Then he turned on Hodges who was leaning against the desk. Hodges took off his hat and shook water out of his hair.

'*Whooee*,' he chuckled. 'Damn rain. See I ain't too keen on water.'

'Never mind that,' Peckard said. 'What kind of fool stunt was that you just pulled? Don't we have enough trouble without you causin' more.'

Hodges glanced at a grinning McCall and made a face. He said, 'I sure didn't do it for fun. I thought you might be interested to know that Temple has skipped town.'

'*What?*' Peckard snapped.

'Yep. Temple, Dutch Canfield, Burt Nels, and Hal Weston. I seen 'em ride off. From back of the King High. Just when all the shootin' began.'

'We sure did underestimate that

feller,' McCall remarked.

Ballard moved over to the desk and began to reload his rifle. His face was a grim set mask.

As if in sudden sympathy with the feelings of the jail's occupants the rain increased its intensity, lashing against the walls with renewed fury.

12

An occasional slug smacked against the outer wall of the jail as the four men inside stood in a momentary deadlock of decision.

'The hell with it,' Ballard snapped. 'I ain't going to let Temple get away a second time.'

Peckard put down his rifle and pushed his hat to the back of his head. There was a frown on his face as he said, 'I know how you feel, son, but it ain't going to do anybody any good if you go off half-cocked.'

'Sheriff's right, Chet,' McCall said. 'We'll get Temple. First we got to settle up with the trigger-happy gents outside before we take off after the big fish.'

For a while it seemed as though Ballard had taken no heed at McCall's suggestion. Then he gave a deep sigh and shook his head.

'Man gets so taken by a thing he has to do he hates to let go of it,' he said.

A window shattered as a well-placed slug tore through it. The lead hammered into the back wall of the jail.

'They're gettin' close,' McCall observed.

'And we damn well can't get out of this place,' Peckard snapped. 'The feller who built this jail ought to be in it. First jail I ever saw that has no back door.'

McCall was making a close inspection of the building's structure. He paused beside the small side-window set in the jail's west wall. Pushing it open he shoved his head out into the narrow alley between the jail and the next building. He pulled his head back in dripping rain-water like a huge shaggy dog fresh out of a creek.

'Reckon you could get through here?' he asked Ballard.

'What you aiming to do?' Peckard inquired.

'If Chett and me can get round the back of the King High and kind of make things unpleasant for them gents,

111

I think we might just about come out on top.'

'Sounds okay.' Peckard grinned. 'Beats anything I can think of so you better go ahead. Me and Dicken will keep 'em busy this end.'

'Sure enough,' Hodges said. He raised an object he held in his hand. In the confusion before no-one had noticed it. Now they saw it was a .50 caliber Sharps buffalo rifle.

'God,' Ballard said, 'if you get a direct hit on the saloon with that, we won't have to bother about pickin' up the pieces.'

McCall shoved his big frame through the window opening. He took the two rifles that Ballard handed him. By the time Ballard joined him, McCall was soaked to the skin by the torrential rain. Just before they moved off Peckard leaned out of the window.

'Watch yourselves,' he said.

'Will do,' Ballard replied.

With McCall in the lead the Texans moved out. They made their way around to the rear of the jail and then along the Gunner Creek back lots. Through the steady hiss of the rain they heard the crack of Peckard' a rifle and the heavier boom of Hodges' Sharps.

'We should be far enough down, now,' McCall said after what seemed an eternity of trampling and slithering about in ankle-deep mud. 'Reckon we can get across the street and around back of the saloon without being seen'?'

Ballard gave a soaked shrug. 'One way of finding out,' he said.

'Okay, Big Bend, let's make like Indians.'

⋆ ⋆ ⋆

For a time there was only pain and darkness. Then slowly the pain lessened and the darkness became a hazy gray film before his eyes. His senses returned gradually until he was fully conscious and the memory of what had happened came to him.

Rio remembered standing at Temple's desk and seeing Temple aiming a gun at him. He had tried to draw his own but had been too slow. Temple's gun had fired and he had felt the impact of the slug. Then Temple had fired again, the force of this slugs knocking him backwards over the desk. He hit the floor hard. Then he had blacked out.

Rio sat up carefully. He leaned against the firm support of the desk and shook his head to clear away the dizziness that seemed to be clinging to him Somewhere he thought he could hear gunfire. Ignoring the pain Rio twisted himself into a position that enabled him to inspect his wounds. One of Temple's slugs had hit him just beneath his ribs, on the right side, lodging somewhere deep in his body. The second slug had torn a piece of flesh from the inside of his upper right arm. Both wounds had bled heavily.

Taking his time Rio clawed his way to his feet, using the desk as a support. He felt weak and the room spun before his eyes. By the time he was upright his face was ashen and dripping with sweat. Keeping his left hand over his side wound, Rio drew his Colt and began to move slowly in the direction of the door. It took him a long time. He had to prop himself up against the wall for a while to stop from collapsing. When he felt able to move he opened the door and stepped out into the corridor.

Now, the sound of gunfire was loud and hard to his ears. It came from down in the saloon and beyond, out in the street.

As Rio headed unsteadily for the stairs he heard a sound that caused him to stop. At the far end of the corridor was the door that opened onto the saloon's rear staircase. And someone was using that staircase. Someone in a big hurry. Rio's thumb pulled back the hammer of his Colt.

Wood splintered, the lock buckling as the door was struck again and again. It swung open, slamming back against the wall, hanging at an angle from one torn hinge.

Rifle in hands Chett Ballard stood framed in the doorway. Coming up behind Ballard was Jess McCall.

All of Rio's hate boiled up inside him in the instant he saw Ballard — a battered and rain-soaked figure. He leveled his gun and triggered off a shot that pounded a chunk of wood out of the wall close to Ballard's head.

Ballard dropped to his knees, swinging up his rifle, firing from the hip. His slug missed. From behind Ballard, McCall, who had that fraction of a second longer to aim, loosed off two slugs that smashed into Rio's body with stunning force.

Rio's gun fell from his numb fingers as he was spun backwards. He came up against the railing that edged the balcony. For a scant second he seemed to freeze in a grotesque pose, his arms flung wide, his face a mask of pain and terror. Then he was gone over the railing. His body swept down in a slow arc. He struck a card table before his broken body hit the saloon floor.

By the time Ballard and McCall reached the railing, Rio was lying motionless amongst the splintered wreckage of the table.

'He was mean enough not to die,' McCall said.

From somewhere below a rifle roared and the sing tore a chunk of wood from the railing. The Texans stepped swiftly away from the edge.

Above the unbroken rattle of gunfire a man's voice could be heard shouting: 'Hey, they're comin' in the back way! Somebody got Rio!'

'I hate a loose mouth!' McCall chided.

He flopped onto his belly and crawled forward so he could see through the railing. Ballard followed suit and they were in time to see three men crowding round Rio's body. McCall recognized two of them as the bouncers he had fought with in the street, before Quince had turned it into something far more serious than a free-for-all. For a moment he reflected on the series of fast and violent events that had taken place since then.

Then he poked his rifle through the railings and let go with a shot that dropped one of the men with a slug through his left leg. The downed man's companions replied with a vicious outburst of firing that sent slugs howling up at Ballard and McCall.

The saloon's interior shook with the blast of heavy guns as the two groups of men triggered off shots with rapidity and in some cases accuracy.

When the firing ceased the two gunslingers had joined their wounded companion on the floor. They were both dead.

McCall was nursing a burnt thumb obtained by placing it on his hot rifle barrel.

Downstairs, out of sight of the Texans, a window smashed. The gunfire still continued. It sounded as if it were coming from the street in front of the saloon. Above the roar of rifles came the heavy boom of, a Sharps .50 caliber.

'Hey, that sounds like Hodges.' McCall sprang to his feet and made a headlong plunge down the stairs with Ballard close behind. On the saloon floor McCall went through tables and chairs like a rampaging longhorn. Going through the batwing doors he almost repeated his earlier stunt. This time, though, he was on his feet when he hit the street.

It was all over.

In the churned mud of Gunner Creek's main street lay three sprawled bodies. Two wore gaping holes in their chests, the result of Dicken Hodges and his Sharps. The third had a smaller but equally bloody wound caused by a slug from Ernie Peckard's Winchester. On the boardwalk lay two more dead men.

And another man was leaning against the hitching-rail clutching a hand to his shattered left shoulder. McCall took all this in with a sweeping glance. He saw

Peckard move forward, saw the wet patch of blood soaking through the cloth of the Sheriff's pants over the left knee. Dropping his rifle, McCall took three steps towards the lawman and caught him in his arms as Peckard began to fall.

'He alright?' Hodges asked.

'He will be,' McCall said. 'Go get the doctor, Dicken, and fetch him over to the hotel.'

Hodges turned and headed through the rain.

Ballard came out of the saloon, pushing before him the man McCall had shot in the leg. He saw McCall with Peckard.

'What happened, Jess?' he asked in a voice edged with concern.

'He caught a slug in the leg. Looks like it might be a bad one.'

'You see to him,' Ballard said. 'I'll get this mess cleared up.'

McCall turned and made for the hotel. He moved easily through the mud, as though he didn't have Peckard's weight in his arms at all.

While all this happened the rain continued to fall without pause, and beside the still bodies, the soft mud was stained a dirty pink as blood and water mingled, finally being washed away as more rain fell on a silent town of violence and death.

13

The rain continued falling for the rest of the day and throughout the night. By the time the sun began to rise, wiping the last stars from the cold gray sky, the downpour had slackened. And when Gunner Creek began to stir into life the rain had stopped completely.

One of the first to rise was Jess McCall. He came out of the jail and stood on the edge of the boardwalk. He gave a weary yawn as he stretched his huge frame. An expression of disgust crossed his unshaven face as he realized he still wore the same clothes as yesterday. The rain-soaked and mud-splattered pants and shirt clung to his body like a burr on a mule's back.

McCall suddenly found that he itched every which-place.

Things had been so upside down yesterday, McCall reflected, that he'd had no time to think about his personal problems. What with Ernie Peckard stopping a slug with his knee, then the rounding up of the remaining Temple crew and getting them behind bars, it had been dark before they'd been able to quit, even though Dicken Hodges had thrown in with Ballard and McCall.

After seeing to Peckard's leg the town's doctor, a tall, tired man called Burkett, had tended the wounds of the men in the cells. He was packing his bag when Chet Ballard had said, 'Doc?'

Burkett had turned and glanced at him. Then he'd gone on with his packing. Finally he'd said, 'I know what you're going to ask. I'll save you the trouble. The bullet that hit Ernie's leg shattered the kneecap beyond repair. He'll get well. But he won't ever bend that leg again. He'll be able to walk, but I don't think he'll do much riding.'

Burkett had put on his hat and coat and left the office. As the door closed behind Burkett it had been pushed open again and McCall had come in, followed by two men Ballard didn't know. Hodges had brought up the rear.

'Put 'em with their kin,' McCall had told Hodges. 'One's the house dealer from the King High, the other's the bartender. Found 'em, hiding out in the saloon. Don't know how deep they're involved so they can stop here until everything gets set right way up again,' he'd explained.

Ballard had nodded. Then he had told McCall what Burkett had said about Peckard.

'Man, that's rough,' McCall had said. 'Hell, Peckard ain't goin' to like it much. He ain't the kind to go hoppin' around on a stick.'

Ballard had agreed with McCall's statement. Both of them shared the inbred independence of men who lived active lives. An independence that rebelled at anything that threatened to halt or hinder it's freedom.

Now as he stood on the boardwalk, McCall recalled his words of not so long ago. Recalled them with a sudden jolt.

Coming towards the jail, from the hotel, was Ernie Peckard. Moving slowly, painfully, with the aid of a stick, the old man came up to McCall. Peckard's face was pale and drawn. He had dark rings beneath his eyes, but they held a stubborn glint of pride that said the fight is still on.

'Morning, Sheriff,' McCall said.

'Don't look at me like that,' Peckard snapped.

'Like what?' McCall inquired pleasantly.

Peckard gave an exasperated snort. 'As if you expect me to drop down dead when the first wind blows. Boy, I got enough in me to outrun you yet.'

McCall grinned. He followed Peckard into the jail. On the far from comfortable cot Dicken Hodges lay snoring loudly in his sleep. Over by the cells Ballard dozed in a chair, his rifle well out of the reach of any of the prisoners. Peckard took all this in then eased himself into his chair behind his desk, his wounded leg stretched out.

'For Hannah's sake, wake up that bellyaching old son!' he said.

McCall stepped across to the cot and put his foot on the edge. He put his weight down and the cot spilled over, tipping Hodges to the floor. Ballard woke up at the noise, in time to see a grinning McCall pick up a swearing Hodges and set him on his feet.

'Goddamn you, boy,' Hodges was saying, 'that's no way to wake a man from a deep sleep. Why, a shock like that could do a lot of damage to a man's brain.'

'Maybe so,' Peckard said. 'You think you can do some riding today, Dicken?'

'After Temple?' Hodges asked. Peckard nodded and Hodges said, 'Hell, I'm on my way.'

Peckard leaned back in his chair and moved his leg. A sheen of sweat glistened on his face.

'You alright?' Ballard asked.'

'No,' Peckard replied. 'This damn leg

hurts like hell. But at the moment there're more important things to worry about.' He turned to Hodges. 'Dicken, go get three mounts and supplies and fetch them to the front of the jail.'

Hodges went out of the office and headed for the livery stable.

'If we three are going after Temple, who is going to keep an eye on the prisoners?' McCall asked.

'Hell, there you go again! I ain't exactly crippled. Anyhow, I reckon I can find someone to give me a hand.' Peckard took off his hat and dropped it on the desk. 'About Temple. I can't give you much help, I'm afraid. But I reckon he's headed South. You watch yourselves, now. Temple's a queer feller. Keep your eyes open all the time. And if you do catch him you better be awake. Once Hodges picks up some sign you'll be all right.'

'I wish I had as much confidence on that score,' McCall said soulfully.

Fifteen minutes later Peckard stood

outside the jail and watched the three horsemen moving slowly across the flats beyond town. The land lay fairly flat here, not changing much until it began to rise where it formed the south wall of the valley.

Before he went back into the jail Peckard gazed along the street.

The town had a scrubbed, cleaned out look about it today. The air smelled fresh, too. Folk beginning to move along the boardwalks had an air of ease about them that he hadn't seen in a long time. Some of them, though, still hadn't realized the meaning of the recent events. They still walked in the shadow of a now destroyed fear that had hung over them for a long time. The town's rebirth had been violent and bloody, but it had been achieved. And the scar would heal in time.

Peckard turned towards the flats beyond town. He shaded his eyes with his hat. The three riders were already out of his sight.

'Luck,' he said softly, then turned

and went back into the jail.

McCall, bringing up the rear, guided his horse around a particularly muddy strip of ground and eased his big frame in the saddle. With them moving out so soon he hadn't had time to get a change of clothing. The rapidly rising sun was beginning to throw down its probing rays and McCall began to feel distinctly uncomfortable.

Just ahead Ballard had his own problems. The horse he rode, a big dun, was in a vile mood. But the Texan was not in the best of spirits himself and gave the dun as good as it handed out.

Dicken Hodges rode about a quarter of a mile in front, roving about as he searched for tracks. Though he'd said that he didn't expect much until they were further out.

The three moved south at a smooth, unhurried pace. Around them the land was for the most part a sweeping expanse of grass, with an occasional clump of bush. Mostly it was grass, and more grass. McCall and Ballard, both, realized, with the inbred instinct of cattle-men, why the valley was such good cow-country. With graze like this, a man could raise a fine herd.

They'd been riding for two hours when Hodges took off his hat and waved it above his head.

Ballard spoke for the first time since they had left town as he acknowledged Hodges' signal. He said: 'Let's hope he's got something.'

The Texans let their mounts run as they headed for the spot where Hodges had dismounted. Hodges was on his knees when they reined in beside him.

'Looks like our lucky day,' he said, indicating a group of hoof-prints in the moist earth.

'You reckon they're the right ones?' asked McCall.

'Made by four horses going south. I reckon they're the real McCoy.'

'Can you follow them from these?' Ballard asked as he gazed toward the distant hills.

Hodges stood up, scratching beneath

his left arm. 'Yep,' he answered.

'They've got a hell of a lead on us,' McCall said,

'Don't mean nothin',' Hodges put in. He mounted up and swung around to face McCall. 'They got 'bout twelve hours on us, I agree. But they ain't in too good a condition for hard riding. They've been living in town too long. Gone soft. And it takes a good man to hide his tracks in country like this. I don't think Temple is smart enough to fool me. No, sir!'

'You think maybe they didn't ride last night? Made camp and then lit out come daylight?' McCall asked.

Hodges nodded, then grinned. 'You ain't so dumb, are you, son? he said. 'I reckon if we make the top of the south wall by noon, we'll be able to rest a while 'til the sun cools off a mite, then keep going the rest of the day and all night. That way we'll make up the time we're behind on.'

'Let's go,' Ballard said, and kneed his horse into motion.

McCall settled his hat firmly on his head and swung in line behind Hodges.

For the next few hours they maintained a steady pace that ate up the miles but didn't exhaust the horses. Above them the sky cleared, with no clouds and a hot sun. The heat increased steadily throughout the morning, drying up the moisture of the previous day's storm, turning the ground hard and dry.

It was just after mid-day when they reached the crest of the southern hills. The climb had been smooth and easy for Hodges had led them up a trail he'd used many times before.

While Ballard and McCall gave the horses and gear a check, Hodges cast around for further tracks. He vanished from their sight for over an hour. Then he came back as silently as he had gone.

He had found the spot where four men had camped for the night in the shadow of a huge outcropping rock. He had seen the ashes of their fire and the place where they had tethered their mounts.

'They headed out about six hours ago,' he said. 'I found their tracks. They won't be hard to follow now.'

They rested for a couple of hours. They ate some dried beef and swilled it down with water. It was a great deal cooler when they mounted up and set off again. Hodges led them along the top of the hills until he picked up the sign he had found. Then they began the descent to the wild and empty vastness of the Kansas plain.

Hodges led the way with the Texans close behind. McCall was rolling himself a cigarette as he rode. Ballard sat his saddle erect and watchful, his eyes on the sweeping expanse of the land ahead.

14

About the time Ballard, McCall, and Dicken Hodges were descending from the top of the Gunner Valley hills, Wade Temple was draining the last of the water from his canteen. His dry throat was barely moistened by the minute trickle of warm liquid.

Temple swore beneath his breath as he hung the empty canteen on his saddle. He was ready to give every last dollar he owned for some good fresh water. Then he shook his head angrily. At the moment the lack of water was his most insignificant problem.

Turning his head he gazed down towards the ground where Burt Nels stood. At Nels' feet lay a dead horse. The animal had put its right foreleg into a pothole and fallen. On trying to get the animal to its feet again, Nels had found that the leg was broken.

Reluctantly he had shot the horse.

This turn of events hadn't done anything to calm down Temple's ravaged nerves. He was tired and thirsty, as well as being dirty and almost at his wits' end. The previous night had been spent out in the driving rain. For their meals they had eaten beans, swilling them down with foul black coffee. They had ridden as soon as it became light, and hadn't stopped until now. This wasn't the way Temple had planned it, and it worried him. He found himself looking back over the way they had come. But he saw nothing except the vast plain that lay baking beneath an unmerciful sun.

So to relieve his frustration and anger he turned on the unfortunate Nels. Temple's voice was forced and biting as he said, 'What now?'

Nels glanced up, running his tongue over his dry lips. His face was scraped raw down the left side, a result of his fall.

'Reckon I'll have to ride double 'til

we can find me another horse,' he said.

'Oh, fine,' Temple snapped. 'That's going to slow us up damn good.' He glanced at Dutch Canfield who gave a short shrug of his shoulders.

'I don't see any other way,' Hal Weston said sharply. He put out a hand and took Nels' saddlebags and rifle. Then he slid his right foot from the stirrup to allow Nels to mount up behind, him.

Temple looked across at Dutch. He kept his eyes firmly on the man as he said, 'There's a way.' And as he spoke he brushed the tips of his fingers across the butt of his holstered gun.

He was counting on an instinct that was telling him Dutch would act as was expected of him. Dutch had already betrayed the men back in Gunner Creek. Temple rationalized that Dutch would do it again, if and when the situation ever arose.

Temple's instinct served him well.

A minute flicker of a nod was Dutch's only indication that he had read the meaning of Temple's glance. Then he acted without warning or hesitation. With the same deliverance that a man uses to kill an insect he drew his gun. The barrel lined up on Nels' back and the hammer clicked back. Then the Colt roared and belched flame as Dutch fired twice.

Nels was almost mounted when the two slugs slammed into him. He was tossed over the horse's back and pitched face down in the dust. Blood welled from the closely spaced holes in his shirt.

For a moment Hal Weston sat rigid in his saddle. Then he jerked his head round toward Dutch who was returning his gun to its holster.

'Dutch,' he yelled, 'have you gone loco? What in hell do you mean gunning' Burt?'

Temple swung his mount alongside Weston's.

'Look, Weston,' he said, 'we had no choice. If you look at it my way you'll see I'm right. If we'd had to ride double it would slow us up a great deal, and it would tire the horses a lot faster, too. We've got a long way to go. God knows how long it'll be until we get a chance to obtain fresh horses and supplies. Think about a posse on our back trail. If my scheme didn't work as I hoped it would, we most probably *are* being chased. So we're going to need all the speed we can get out of these animals. And riding double wouldn't be the way to do it.'

Temple swung away from Weston and moved out. Dutch followed him without a backward glance.

Hal Weston remained where he was for a while. He seemed to be fighting some inner conflict. Finally he ran his hand across his face. Before he rode off he gave a last look at the body of Burt Nels. Then he swung his horse's head round and galloped after Temple and Dutch.

The noise of their departure rapidly faded into the distance and there was only the silence and the heat.

It was late afternoon when Dicken Hodges reined in his horse a few yards from the body of Burt Nels. He turned in his saddle and waved for Ballard and McCall to join him. Then he dismounted and knelt by the body.

'Who is it?' Ballard asked as he came alongside.

Hodges stood up. 'Name of Nels,' he paid.

'Looks like he got it in the back from here,' McCall said from the saddle. 'Wonder what happened?'

'You can ask Temple when we find him,' Ballard said.

'Yeah, I'm sure.'

'We'd better bury this poor devil,' Hodges said.

★ ★ ★

A quarter-of-an-hour later they mounted up and headed out again. Behind them they left a long, narrow mound of earth and stones, the final resting place for Burt Nels.

They rode steadily until night began to fall. Twenty minutes for a cold meal and a rest for the horses then they were in the saddle again and heading into the darkness.

Their pace was slowed until the moon rose big and bright in the heavens. With the darkness came the sharp, biting cold of the open plain, and they paused to put on the thick, short-coats that Hodges had insisted they bring.

As they struggled into the heavy coats Hodges said, 'I reckon if we keep moving' all night, we'll catch up with 'em sometime tomorrow. Like I said before, Temple and his boys are town rats, not the prairie kind. They can't move in the dark like me.'

McCall blew on his chilled hands. 'Hell, you got to admit that there's something to living in a town. A night like this a man needs a place he can go to get a drink. Man, what would I give for a bottle of good whisky.'

Hodges gave a toothy grin as he

rummaged about in the pouch of his worn saddlebags. His hand rose to the accompaniment of a familiar sound. That of liquid swilling about inside a bottle.

'This feller is my kind of man,' McCall said as he took the bottle.

After McCall's healthy swallow of its contents the bottle passed to Ballard, then back to Hodges. The old man took a mouthful then replaced the cork.

'I feel like riding none-stop to Juarez after that,' Ballard said as the whisky cut a path clear down to his boot heels. 'What was that stuff?'

' 'Bout as crude as it comes,' Hodges grunted.

'Seems to have quieted down Texas, here,' Ballard grinned.

McCall was holding a hand to his stomach and waiting for the whisky to settle before he moved. He finally gave a deep sigh and said, 'That was downright lethal stuff. All I want now is a pretty gal and I'll be the happiest man in Kansas.'

Hodges gave a low chuckle. 'I carried some queer stuff in my bags,' he said, 'but it never run to women.'

'Don't fret none,' McCall said. 'I'll make do with my thoughts.'

He sighed wistfully and kneed his horse forward.

Hodges rode ahead again and a grinning Ballard brought up the rear.

Throughout the night they kept up the steady pace that didn't tire the horses but got them a long way before the graying sky heralded dawn. The sun rose to reveal a change in the landscape. Where yesterday had been a wide expanse of grassland, the scene now was of undulating hills and ravines, hard baked earth and rocks with occasional clumps of stunted scrub.

As they reined in atop a rise McCall said: 'I never knew country to change so rapidly.'

'It gets worse further out,' Hodges said.

They moved out in silence. Hodges concentrated on following the tracks that were bringing them nearer their quarry.

The sun was well up when, as they halted to remove their coats, McCall saw them. No more than a quarter-of-a-mile away. Three horsemen They went out of sight behind some rocks for a few seconds, then he saw them again. McCall brought his mount up beside Ballard's.

'Up ahead,' he said.

'I see 'em. Dicken?'

Hodges nodded. 'Yep. Got 'em.'

'Any suggestions as how we catch 'em?' McCall asked.

'Forget any ideas that include surprising them,' Ballard said

Hodges and McCall turned and saw the three riders sitting their now motionless mounts. It was obvious that they had spotted their pursuers. Then they wheeled their horses around and headed out at a gallop.

'Damn,' McCall said.

Ballard kicked his horse into motion and it leapt forward eagerly. Hodges and McCall followed closely, their mounts moving forward in the first hard riding they'd done since leaving Gunner Creek.

It was Temple who spotted the three men on horseback. He had been taking frequent glances along the back-trail ever since they had left Burt Nels beside his dead horse the previous day.

Now as he saw the three, sitting their mounts on a rise, he felt an icy hand clutch at his heart. It was the one thing he'd been praying for not to happen. He couldn't recognize any of the men. Somehow, though, he knew without doubt that one of them would be Chet Ballard.

Temple reined in his sweating horse and dropped a hand to loosen his gun.

'Dutch,' he called, 'we've got company.' He tried to sound calm, but didn't think he'd succeeded.

Both Dutch and Hal Weston reined in alongside of Temple. They stared across the stretch of hot, dusty earth that lay between them and their pursuers.

'Looks like your scheme didn't work after all,' Dutch said.

'They haven't got us yet,' Temple snapped back.

Weston said, 'If it comes to making a run we won't get far on these mounts. They're about finished.'

'Then we'll make a fight,' Dutch said. 'Get in amongst some of these rocks and pick 'em off when they come in range.'

Temple opened his mouth to protest, then thought better of it. He realized that Dutch's way was the only one left open to them. His horse was practically exhausted and wouldn't carry him far if it had to race. No matter how he turned this was one time in his life he was going to have to stand and fight if he wanted to keep alive.

With Dutch leading the way they moved out fast. Dutch headed for a sprawling bed of jumbled rock that lay ahead. It would make an ample defensive position for what they were planning.

They had to dismount and lead the horses as the ground became rougher and strewn with chunks of hard, jagged stone. As they moved deeper into the rock-bed the chunks of stone became boulders, then vast, towering masses of solid, sun-bleached rock.

They halted at a point which gave them protection, yet allowed a clear view of the land spread out before their eyes. Hal Weston led their horses into the cover of a huge boulder. He rejoined Temple and Dutch. They all had their rifles. Dutch took his and climbed up onto a boulder, lying on his stomach, his rifle ready for when the three riders came into sight over a rise about a hundred yards from where he lay.

Below, in the shade of a smaller boulder, Temple crouched down and wiped sweat from his face. He made a futile attempt to brush away some of the dirt from his soiled clothing.

Irritably he ran his hands over his smarting eyes and unshaven chin.

Dutch suddenly said, '*They're comin*'!'

The rattle of lever-actions being worked brought Temple to his feet. Keeping low he looked over the top of his protecting boulder, Hal Weston beside him.

He saw the riders as they appeared over the rise a hundred yards away.

'You recognize them?' he asked.

'It's that McCall feller, old Dicken Hodges . . . and Ballard,' Dutch replied.

'Hell, with that old bastard, Hodges, trackin' it's no wonder they found us,' Weston said.

'Well he won't do any more trackin',' Dutch snapped. He raised his rifle and took swift aim. When he fired the boom of his gun slammed and rolled around the rocks for a long time.

'Hey, you got the bastard,' Weston said viciously.

As he spoke one of the riders slid from his horse and fell stiffly to the ground. Instantly the other two left their saddles and threw themselves onto the hard earth.

* * *

Dust flew up and created a hazy curtain the hot air as Hodges' horse picked its sure-footed way amongst the rock and scrub. Ballard and McCall bringing up the rear were covered in a choking mist as the powder — fine dust swirled over them.

McCall couldn't express his feelings on the matter. If he had opened his mouth he would have been eating dirt. So he put his head down and pulled his hat low.

Their pace had been slowed to a swift walk, for it was too risky to push the horses in this kind of terrain. A man on foot wouldn't last long out here and riding a horse recklessly amongst these jagged rocks and rutted slopes of iron-hard earth was one sure way of ending up like that.

'Hold up,' Hodges said suddenly.

McCall reined in beside Hodges. 'See 'em?' he asked.

Hodges shook his head. 'Nope. But I reckon they're up ahead. In them rocks.'

'They sure couldn't pick a better place,' Ballard said. He placed his hands on the saddle-horn and eased his weight in the saddle. His bruised face was dust-grimed and weary. 'If they're as tired as me and my horse they'll be in there.'

McCall said, 'We'd better get the hell out of sight before they start shootin' then.'

His words had hardly been spoken when there came the sharp, vicious crack of a rifle from somewhere in the rocks up ahead. Then came the smack of lead against flesh.

Hodges gave a grunt of pain and began to topple sideways. Blood ran freely from the hole in his chest, making a big stain on the front of his buckskin shirt. Before either of the Texans could move he had slipped from his horse and sprawled face down on the ground.

Ballard was the first to move. He gave McCall a shove. 'Get down!' he yelled. They rolled from their saddles and bellied down onto the hot earth.

McCall wriggled over to where Ballard lay beside Hodges.

'How is he?' he asked.

Ballard shook his head, his mouth a narrow line. Behind almost closed lids his eyes burned like cold hard diamonds.

'The bastards,' McCall said softly. He glanced at Hodges' still body. 'Poor old Dicken. Didn't have a chance.'

'You can expect that kind of treatment from Temple and his crew. Don't give the other feller a chance in hell. Wait until he's got his back to you, then let him have it.' Ballard drew his Colt and checked the cylinder. 'Maybe it's about time he was paid back the same way he's been dealing.'

'We'd better get some cover first,' McCall said tightly. 'With all respect to Dicken, I don't want to be caught with *my* pants down.'

Together they worked their way down to the bottom of the slope until they were safe from any hidden rifleman in the rocks.

Ballard pulled off his hat and dropped it on the ground beside him. Then he removed his gun belt.

'You planning something?' McCall inquired.

Nodding, Ballard removed his Colt from its holster. Then he glanced up. 'We could spend all day waiting for them to make a move,' he said. 'So I'm going to start the show. You keep their attention over here, and I'll work my way round and come in from their rear.'

McCall scratched the back of his neck. 'You quite sure you want to do it this way?'

'I'm sure,' Ballard said. 'Why?'

'I wouldn't like to think maybe I'd let you go and dig your own grave.'

'I know what you mean, Jess,' Ballard said. 'This is no wild stunt. I want Temple too much to do anything crazy.'

'Okay. How long do you reckon it'll take to get round then?'

'Hard to say. One maybe two hours. Reckon you can keep 'em busy that long?'

'I'll do it if I have to stand up a throw rocks at 'em,' McCall grinned.

Ballard shoved his Colt into the top of his pants and began to move along the bottom of the ridge. He intended to get well clear of the rock bed before he made his swing around to the rear.

Jess McCall watched him go, not moving until Ballard was out of sight. Then he crawled to the top of the ridge again. A sudden movement caused him to snatch for his gun. But it was only one of the horses. The animal had stayed at the top of the ridge when their riders had left them. Remembering the rifles the horses carried, McCall reached up and made a grab for the reins. For a moment his head was showing above the crest of the ridge. As McCall's fingers curled around the reins there came a sudden outburst of rifle fire. Slugs whipped over his head in a deadly rain. With startled snorts the three horses began a panicked, slithering descent of the slope. McCall was dragged behind then until he let go of the reins. He pulled himself upright and slapped the dust from his clothes. He saw that the horses had come to a nervous stop, standing close together. He closed in and took the two rifles and the big .50 caliber Sharps that Dicken Hodges had put to deadly use back in Gunner Creek. From the pouch in Hodges' saddlebags he found a box of cartridges for the Sharps. With his collection of weapons McCall made his way back up the slope. This time he was a whole lot more careful. He removed his battered hat before he peered over the top.

His first inspection of the rock bed revealed nothing. He saw only the sprawling jumble of gray-white boulders which seemed to spread for a long way. There was no movement and, now the shooting had stopped, no sound.

He noticed that at once. It was that strange silence that is only found in a vast, empty space such as this. It was a silence so acute that it could almost be heard. And it irritated McCall.

'We can put that right, too,' he said darkly as he levered a round into the breech of his own Winchester. Raising it to his shoulder he lined it up with a distant boulder and pulled the trigger. The Winchester nudged his shoulder as it spat out the slug. McCall heard the whine of the slug as it slapped the rock and then howled off into the blue. Swinging the muzzle round a little McCall triggered off a couple more shots.

Suddenly there came an answering shot from amongst the rocks. The slug nicked the left sleeve of McCall's shirt.

'Thanks, friend,' McCall said, for he had seen the puff of powder smoke from the rifle.

Now he began to concentrate his fire on that particular spot.

15

Heat, dust, and the slow crablike crawl he was forced to employ made Chet Ballard's journey nerve-wracking and unpleasant. The back of his shirt stuck to his sweating flesh and his whole body itched violently. The palms of his hands were raw from sliding against the rough, sharp rocks. The fact that the sun was making the rocks almost untouchable didn't help any.

After endless minutes of painful progress Ballard stopped and rolled into the shade of the nearest rock. In the distance he could hear the sound of gunshots. McCall had opened up within a short time of Ballard's departure and had kept up a steady rate of fire ever since.

Reluctantly, Ballard pushed away from the rock and resumed his slow circling of the rock-bed. It was a monotonous tack made that much more depressing by the thought that if Temple and his companions realized that they were being fired at by only one man, they would catch on very quickly. And when he, Ballard, arrived expecting to surprise them, he would find he was on the receiving end of a lead-filled welcome.

Time was his enemy at the moment. It was time he needed, but knew he didn't have.

Ballard reckoned he had been moving for well over an hour when he slid onto the top of a tall boulder. It had been a struggle but he had finally managed to get there. Now he lay flat on his stomach and gazed thankfully down on the scene he'd been hoping to see.

Three hundred yards ahead he could see his goal. Behind a large boulder stood three weary horses, their heads low. A few yards to one side were three men. One was spread out on top of a high rock while the other two were positioned behind a lower but broader slab of rock. All three men were firing spasmodically towards the spot where Jess McCall lay.

Ballard's job now was to get as close to the three men as was possible in the shortest time he could make. He saw there was ample cover, and the slight amount of noise he might make would be drowned by the sound of the firing guns. As he slid down off his rock, Ballard cautioned himself to keep low in case a stray slug should come his way.

He drew his .45 from his pants and checked the chamber again. *Six shots and the element of surprise might just do the trick*, he thought. *It'll be the last-post for this Texas boy if it goes wrong.*

Ballard began to move forward. He kept his eyes on the figures of the three men up ahead, his gun ready for use if one should turn and spot him before he was close enough to spring his trap.

'Keep them busy a few more minutes, Jess,' he said softly.

★ ★ ★

Hal Weston swore loudly as a rifle slug howled off the rock close to his face. Sharp stone chips stung his cheek.

'One of them bastards has got me in his sights,' he yelled, wiping at the blood coursing down his face.

'Move then,' Dutch called from his own position.

'Like hell,' Weston snapped. 'I ain't puttin' my head anywhere it can be shot off.'

Rifle slugs howled overhead at regular intervals, chipping away at the surrounding rocks. Dutch did most of the return fire, being in the best position. He had taken himself to a higher spot, allowing him to shoot down on McCall's position.

'We can't stay here too long,' Temple said. 'We're already low on water and it isn't going to get any better.'

'I know, I know,' Dutch said. He lowered his rifle. 'We need to give the horses time to rest up. Then we can slip

158

out the back way after dark.'

He rolled on his back and checked out the stretch of rocks that lay behind them. He spent some time checking this section out.

Without warning he froze, the expression on his face turning to one of anger. Then he made a grab for his rifle.

'*Behind us. It's Ballard!*'

Temple and Weston spun round.

On a flat boulder no more than twenty feet away stood Chet Ballard. He was caked in dust, hatless, and in his right hand was a raised Colt.

Wade Temple stared at the tall figure, disbelief in his eyes.

'*Get him!*' he screamed wildly. 'I want that bastard dead!' And as he uttered the words he swung up his rifle and started shooting.

McCall was down to his last few rounds. In the past hour he had steadily exhausted his supply. The constant stream of fire he had been maintaining had finally brought him down to three cartridges for the .50 caliber Sharps.

'If you're going to make your play, Chet, make it soon,' he said out loud.

He slid one of the cartridges into the breech of the Sharps and notched back the hammer.

McCall noticed that the firing from Temple's position had ceased. He found out why in the same breath.

A shout from the distant position made McCall search the jumble of rocks. He recognized the tall figure of Chet Ballard outlined against the skyline. It was McCall's cue to act. He pushed to his feet and made a dash for the first scatterings of small stones that marked the beginnings of the sprawling rock formation.

Before he had gone many yards he heard gunshots rip the heavy, heat-laden air.

When Ballard rose upright on the rock, he had been almost ready to congratulate himself on pulling off his plan. Then without warning Dutch Canfield had turned his head and spotted Ballard. Dutch's yell had brought Temple and Weston from lower down.

Wade Temple's face had lost its color completely. It was white, and wet with sweat. The eyes had burned with hate and fear as Temple had stared at Ballard. Temple's wild cry had been followed by a burst of firing from his jerking rifle.

And even as Temple was triggering his rifle, Ballard saw the figure of Jess McCall appear over the top of the rise, behind which he had lain for the past hour, and come running towards the rocks, a rifle in his hands.

16

Out of five shots that Temple fired only one touched the Texan, Ballard felt it burn a furrow across his left hip. He had the presence of mind to drop to one knee, hoping to make as small a target as possible for the guns that were being turned on him.

Hal Weston had his rifle leveled when Ballard's Colt roared twice. Weston gave a hoarse scream and threw his weapon from him. He clasped his hands to his face, blood spurting between his fingers. The force of the heavy slugs knocked him back and he stumbled, fell. He lay on the rock, his body twitching violently, animal like sounds coming from deep in his throat.

A gun fired and the slug ripped a long scar in the rock by the heel of Ballard's left boot. The Texan looked up at Dutch Canfield who was half-standing on his high rock. Ballard snapped off a quick shot that missed. He slapped back the hammer and pulled the trigger again. The Colt didn't fire. It gave only a dull click as the hammer fell on a dud shell.

Dutch was in the act of pulling the trigger of his rifle when a gun went off. It wasn't Ballard's. The Texan recognized it as the big .50 caliber Sharps. The slug hit Dutch in the back and tore its way through his thick body, leaving a gaping hole in his chest. Dutch's body was tossed off the rock like a rag doll. He fell in a curving arc and slammed face down onto the rocks below.

The rattling echo of the Sharps was still being tossed back and forth among the boulders when Ballard spun around towards the spot where he had last seen Wade Temple. Temple was gone. All Ballard saw was the still-jerking body of Hal Weston and the ugly splashes of blood on the smooth rock.

Then off to his left Ballard heard a

horse snort impatiently. He turned, coming to his feet. As he rose he cocked the Colt, hoping for a live cartridge under the hammer this time.

In the shadow of a tall boulder, Wade Temple was mounted on one of the three horses, a pair of bulging saddlebags in his free hand. He was kicking the horse's sides violently as he attempted to get it to move. The horse, though, was nervous after all the shooting, and was near exhaustion too. It pawed the rock frantically, its eyes rolling up until the whites showed.

As Ballard started forward Temple turned his head and saw him, flinging the saddlebags aside. Temple made an even greater effort to get his mount moving. The horse strained and lunged forward, its hooves sliding on the hard surface. It reared up on its hind legs, almost unseating Temple. With only a few feet between them, Ballard threw his gun aside and made a lunge for Temple. His arms circled Temple's waist and dragged him from the saddle.

The two men sprawled on the rock in a thrashing heap.

Ballard got his feet under him and as he rose he dragged Temple upright. Temple had been winded by the fall and he leaned heavily on the Texan's arm. Temple's hair was plastered over his face which was a mask of dust and sweat and stubble.

For a moment Ballard held onto Temple. Then abruptly he swung his huge right fist into Temple's face. Temple was hurled back by the blow and he staggered drunkenly before he fell. Ballard moved in and pulled Temple to his feet again, then once more he slammed his fist at the men's face. As Temple went down again Ballard moved after him.

From somewhere, Temple summoned a reserve of strength that enabled him to roll aside as Ballard bent to grab him. Temple came to his feet and stood watching Ballard. Blood streaked the lower part of Temple's face and his breathing was ragged.

'Just you and me, Temple,' Ballard said softly. 'There's nobody left to do your fighting this time.'

The Texan came at Temple slowly, his hands clenched into huge and deadly fists. Temple looked right and left as if seeking some way of escape. But there was none. Then he remembered the holstered gun he wore and his hand darted for it. But Ballard was on him before the weapon was halfway free of the leather. He chopped at Temple's wrist and the gun dropped from numbed fingers.

Temple gave a ragged moan and lashed out with his left arm. His fist hit Ballard in the mouth, splitting his lips. Again Temple swung, this time his clenched fist slammed into the Texan's stomach. As Ballard reeled back from this sudden and unexpected attack, Temple's fists hammered home some telling pinches. Ballard stumbled and fell to his knees. The heel of Temple's boot buried itself into his stomach and Ballard gagged, pain sweeping up his body in a blinding wave.

Ballard knew he had to get to his feet fast, or he would be dead. Temple was crazed with fear, and it was this fear that was giving him his strength. He was like some wild animal fighting for its life, using every means at it. disposal. Through the pain that fogged his brain, Ballard concentrated every fiber of his being in an effort to get to his feet. He ignored the powerful blows that rained down on his head and shoulders. With a concerted thrust Ballard rose and hurled himself at Temple.

Temple slithered back a few feet, then came forward again. A hard fist smacked into his face and Temple felt blood streaming from his shattered nose. Temple stepped in close and swung a right that stung over Ballard's right eye. Ballard returned with two swift blows to Temple's heart. Temple stepped back with a pained expression. Ballard followed him closely and swung his left fist at Temple's face. Temple knocked the arm aside and swung one of his own, opening a gash over

Ballard's right eye.

Jess McCall suddenly appeared around the boulder from which Dutch Canfield had fallen. He took in the sprawled bodies, then turned to the two men who were locked in a violent and brutal fight that had only one outcome.

Ballard and Temple traded savage, crippling blows with vicious power, neither of them giving or taking an inch. Their faces were almost hidden beneath masks of blood. As McCall watched he realized that this was something between two men who hated each other to the extreme.

A punch to the stomach bent Ballard forward. Temple slammed his fist down hard across the back of Ballard's neck, pitching him forward onto his face.

At this point McCall started forward, raising his rifle. Then he remembered that the weapon was empty. He threw it aside.

Temple moved even faster. Flung himself into the saddle of his horse the moment Ballard went down. His face was taut with fear and rage. With a savage curse he wrenched the horse's head round, kicking hard with his boots. The startled animal, squealing loudly, rolled its eyes and leapt forward. Its hooves skidded and slithered on the rock. Then it regained its balance and sprang forward.

McCall saw the horse move off and leapt towards it, hoping to be able to grab hold of Temple. As the rearing bulk of the horse loomed close he made a lunge. His fingers caught hold of Temple's left boot. But then the horse's side slanted into him, knocking him aside. McCall fell hard, the breath forced from his body.

Temple triumphantly urged the horse onwards. Stones rattled from beneath the clattering hooves.

As the horse and rider vanished from sight behind an outcropping of rock Ballard shoved himself upright. He shook his head violently, trying to dispel the roaring sensation that threatened to split his skull wide open. He began to push himself to his feet, even though his entire body was demanding to be allowed to lie down. When he finally did stand upright he felt sick and giddy. He knew he had to get himself across to one of the horses and mount up. Every second he delayed gave Temple a better chance of escape. After all he'd gone through, and for all the people who'd suffered, he couldn't allow the man to escape. He had come too far and gone through too much to let it end this way. He forced his unsteady legs to carry him across the rock towards the horses. As he reached the nearest one he grabbed the saddle horn. Ballard hung there for a while until his strength built up enough so he could haul himself onto the horse's back.

He was about to move off when there was a tug at his sleeve. Ballard glanced down. McCall stood gazing up at him.

'You want me to come along?' McCall asked. He looked a fearsome sight, with the side of his face scraped raw and bloody from contact with the rough rock.

Ballard shook his head. 'Thanks, Jess, but this is my job. I'd be obliged if you'd let me handle it myself.'

McCall nodded. 'Sure thing. Only you watch out. That *hombre* is *loco*.'

Ballard swung the horse's head round and kicked in his heels. The horse moved off cautiously. Ballard set it on Temple's trail.

Fear, desperation, the will to live. These were the things that caused Wade Temple to throw caution aside in his headlong flight across the rock-bed. Under normal circumstances he would have never even considered riding at such a pace. It was a miracle that the speeding horse didn't fall. Somehow it kept its feet as it clattered across the treacherous surface.

Temple rode in this manner for a full half hour. Then he began to notice that the rock was giving way to easier ground. He realized he was coming to the end of the rock-bed. Shortly, then, the horse crossed the last stretch of rock and its hooves struck dry, powdery earth again.

With a sigh Temple reined in his sweating mount. As he let his taut nerves relax, his head dropping onto his chest. He closed his eyes. He could feel his heart pounding, slanting against his ribs. His face and body ached. As he calmed down, he began to think that maybe he'd come out on top after all. He was alive. He had his money. And he had a horse. Ahead lay open country, and new prospects, challenges. He could make a fresh start, somewhere he wasn't known. He began to feel better. *Hell*, he thought, *things aren't so bad*. His only regret was that he'd been unable to kill Chett Ballard. At the memory of the Texan, his disposition soured a little. But Temple didn't' allow himself to dwell on the subject for long.

He raised his head. *Now was the time for looking ahead*, he told himself. He kicked his mount into motion. As the horse moved off Temple had a quick look at his back trail.

An angry curse burst from his lips as he saw a horse and, rider come into view some distance back. At such a distance Temple couldn't make out the rider's features; but even so he knew it was Chet Ballard. Knew it as sure as he sat his horse.

'Damn you, Ballard,' Temple yelled out loud.

Temple lashed his horse into a gallop. His mind raced as he strove to keep a level head. His only way out was to get far ahead of Ballard and keep it that way.

If only he'd had Ballard dealt with back in Gunner Creek. He wouldn't be running now if he had. *One man*, he thought bitterly, *had ruined his hold over a town*. Had cost him his kingdom, his men, his power. And almost his life. One man. One vengeance-seeking man, with the persistence of a web-spinning spider, and the durability of a grizzly bear. Ballard had slogged and fought his way through every obstacle to get at his enemy. And he was still trying. Temple had the sudden, shocking realization that Ballard would carry on with his pursuit until one of them was dead.

Urged on by this he forced his horse on; the animal was straining its resources to the utmost now. And it was tiring very fast.

The path it was taking led along the bottom of a narrow valley. On both sides the land rose sharply. Temple saw this and realized he might suddenly find himself at a dead end. He swung the horse round and forced it to climb one of the steep valley sides.

The slope underfoot was loose shale. And halfway up the horse stumbled. Unable to regain its balance it reared up, then twisted sideways. Temple threw himself from the saddle, falling to his knees. He heard the horse scream in terror. The animal rolled and slithered down the slope. It thrashed about wildly in a vain attempt to stop its plunging fall. It crashed to a bone jarring stop far down the slope.

Panting heavily, Temple slid down the slope. His hands were raw and bleeding from clawing at the shale. By the time he reached the horse he was gasping for breath. There was a searing, burning pain in his chest. He saw at a glance that the horse was dead. Temple sank to his knees beside the carcass and reached for the money-filled saddlebags. Frustration heaped upon frustration as he saw that one pouch was pinned beneath the dead horse. It was no use trying to move the animal himself. After a few ineffectual tugs at the saddlebags he tore open the exposed pouch and began to transfer the bundles of bills to his pockets.

The sound of pounding hooves came to his ears. Turning, he was in time to see Chet Ballard urging his own horse up the base of the slope.

Grabbing the rest of the money in his arms Temple rose to his feet and began to struggle up the slope. Great panting sobs came from his throat as he stumbled and fell, up the slope. It was a nightmare task. The loose surface made it hard going. His feet kept on slipping. His legs ached.

A glance over his shoulder showed Ballard on foot himself, plunging wildly up the slope. Temple glanced up. The top was close. If he could reach there he might have a chance. Any kind of chance would do.

One of the bundles of bills fell from his arms. Stopping to pick it up Temple dropped another. The retaining band of this one broke and bills blew in every direction. Temple watched the flying bills for a second, then turned and struggled on. More bills fell from his grasp as he struggled on. On his knees he saw a shadow fall across the slope just ahead of him. He spun round. It was Ballard.

In the instant his eyes met Ballard's, Temple saw the Texan as the cause of all his troubles. If it hadn't been for Ballard he would still be in Gunner

Creek, not out here in this empty, hot, wasteland, struggling for his life.

With a tormented scream Temple let go of his money and threw himself at Ballard. As he crashed against the Texan, Temple closed his hands around Ballard's throat. Off balance the two men hurtled backwards and rolled down the slope in a tangle of thrashing arms and legs. Dust billowed up in great thick clouds as they struggled.

Ballard fought to get Temple's hands off his neck. His breath was being choked out of him. His eyes bulged, his head pounded. He could see Temple's face, wild-eyed and twitching, and that face became a blur as his eyes went out of focus. Kicking and twisting Ballard rolled Temple off him as they slid further down the slope. The swirling dust caked them and got into their eyes and mouths, choking and blinding them.

Ballard's clawing hands finally found Temple's wrists. Jerking Temple's hands from his throat Ballard slammed his fist into Temple's face. Blood spurted from split lips.

Temple hooked his foot round and got it against Ballard's stomach. He shoved and the Texan was tossed aside. Temple scrambled to his feet, and Ballard pushed himself upright, too. He moved in on Temple, his fists clenched.

But it was Temple who landed the first blow. A body-jarring punch to the jaw that rocked the big Texan and put him off guard long enough for Temple to land three more punches.

Ballard reeled but stayed on his feet. He tasted blood in his mouth. He saw Temple's fist coming again and blocked it. Then he threw a punch of his own. It opened a two-inch gash on Temple's cheek. Blood streaked hotly down Temple's face. Again Ballard slammed his fist into Temple's face, ignoring the fact that his knuckles were torn.

Temple was almost out on his feet. He swayed drunkenly. His face was an ugly sight now. A mass of swollen, bloody flesh. He made no attempt to fight back. He just held himself upright while Ballard hit him.

Ballard, his strength almost gone, summoned all his strength in a final punch. It was a shattering blow, that landed on the point of Temple's jaw with a loud, solid crack. Temple's head jerked back with a whip-like motion. He fell back, and hit the slope on his side. He twisted and rolled down the slope, almost reaching the bottom. Streams of banknotes fluttered from his pockets, littering the slope in their hundreds.

For a time Ballard didn't move. When he did, he walked down the slope like a man in a trance. He reached Temple and bent over him. The moment he saw the ugly, twisted position of Temple's neck he knew it was all over. Temple was dead.

Ballard's long search was over. He had avenged the deaths of his friends. It made no difference. They were still dead. Nothing would bring them back. But now the score was even. The man who had killed them was dead himself. And Ballard was satisfied.

He sat down beside the body and closed his eyes, let his head fall onto his chest.

He was still in that position when Jess McCall rode up some time later. He had the dead outlaws' horses roped together and following up behind his and Ballard's. McCall surveyed the scene in silence. He dismounted. Crossing over to where Ballard sat he halted, shoved his hat to the back of his head.

'Chet, you alright?' he asked. He had to repeat it twice before Ballard raised his bloody face.

I am now,' he said.

He pushed to his feet.

'I buried Dicken and the other two back there,' McCall said. He glanced down it Temple. 'Reckon we'd better do the same for him.'

Ballard nodded. 'Man should have a grave, no matter what he's done.'

They had no tools so they dug a shallow, hole with their bare hands and the heels of their boots. And when the task was completed they covered the mound with rocks.

'One hell of a lonely place for a man to die,' McCall said.

'I guess when you die, anyplace they put you is lonely,' Ballard said. Between them they removed the saddlebags from the dead horse. Then they collected up as much of the scattered money they could. It was a long job.

Ballard finally said,' 'Let's get away from here.'

They mounted up and rode. They paused, later, beside the grave of Dicken Hodges, long enough for Ballard to pay his respects. Then they headed out.

It was dark when they finally halted and made camp for the night. They had a swift meal, then rolled up in their blankets.

Neither of them felt like talking.

And it took Ballard a long time to get to sleep.

17

Two days later they rode slowly up Gunner Creek's' main street and reined in before the jail. McCall climbed down from his saddle and gazed with tired eyes at the people moving up and down the boardwalks.

'Sure looks different to when we first came,' Ballard said as he dismounted. Behind his own horse stood four other mounts and Ballard waved a hand in their direction. 'I'd better get these over to the livery stable. They need some rest.'

McCall ran a hand over his unshaven face. 'Don't we all,' he said. He handed the reins of his horse over to Ballard.

As Ballard led the horses away McCall stepped up on the boardwalk. Over one arm he carried the two sets of saddlebags that held the money Wade Temple had died for. McCall ignored the curious stares he received from passersby.

Pushing open the door he stepped into the office. As he closed the door a figure rose from behind the desk. It was Phil Lansing. The rancher wore a holstered revolver and had a badge pinned to the front of his shirt. Lansing came round the desk as he recognized McCall.

'You don't look too good,' he said.

McCall took off his hat and threw it on the desk.

'Rough?' Lansing asked.

'Enough that Dicken Hodges didn't make it,' McCall told him.

Lansing shook his head slowly. 'Dicken? *Dead*? God, I never thought I'd live to hear that.'

Depositing the saddlebags on the desk McCall went across to the fresh-water pail and filled the tin cup. He swallowed four cupfuls straight off.

'Where's Ballard?' Lansing asked.

'He took the horses over to the stable.' McCall caught Lansing's questioning expression. 'They're all dead,' he said. 'Temple, Dutch, Nels, Weston.'

'And Dicken,' Lansing added bitterly.

McCall nodded. 'Yeah. Dicken, too.'

For a moment there was an uneasy silence. Then McCall asked: 'I don't see Peckard. Where is he?'

Lansing smiled. 'Doc Burkett finally got Ernie to go to bed and stay there. Ever since you left, Ernie and Burkett have been goin' at it like a couple of wild-men. Doc won in the end, though. I took over here when Ernie asked me. It's the least I could do after what happened.'

'By the way, how's the missus?' McCall inquired.

'It'll take time but we'll get through. Doc Burkett's wife is looking after her over at the Doc's house.'

'How about the characters in the back' McCall asked, waving a hand in the direction of the cells.

'No trouble,' Lansing told him. 'They seem to have lost the urge to fight. Our telegraph is still out of action since the storm, so Ernie got someone to ride to over to Thompson's Crossing and get a message to the U.S. Marshall office in Dodge. So all we have to do now is wait for the law to come and sort the mess out.'

'Well, I'd better go round and see Peckard before he starts in to hoppin' around again.' McCall patted the saddlebags. 'Take good care of these,' he said. 'There's a hell of a pile of cash in then.'

He put on his hat and went out of the office. He headed across the street, making for the hotel at the other end of town. As he stepped up onto the boardwalk Ballard fell in step beside him.

'Where are we going?' he asked McCall.

McCall told him what Lansing had said and Ballard grinned. 'I can imagine Burkett had a hell of a job gettin' Peckard to stop in bed.'

They reached the hotel and walked into the lobby. The skinny desk clerk was talking to a middle-aged, over-dressed woman and, as Ballard and McCall came up to the desk, he glanced at them. His lips drew back in a look of disgust as he took in the filthy state of the Texans and their clothes. He began to speak, then paused as he recognized then.

'Why, Mr. McCall and Mr. Ballard, isn't it? Nice to see you again. What can I do for you?'

'Which is Ernie Peckard's room, 'McCall asked.

'Why it's number four, just at the head of the stairs. Is there anything else I can do for you?'

'Yep. You can get some hot water ready for a bath,' McCall said. 'I smell worse than a pile of buffalo-dung.' The woman gave a feeble moan and put a hand to her mouth. McCall glanced at her. Then he raised his hat. 'Sorry, ma'am, but if you'd ever smelt buffalo-dung you'd know I was right.'

McCall followed Ballard up the stairs. At the top they found number four and Ballard knocked on the door. From inside the room Peckard's voice yelled, 'Come in, damn you, I ain't comin' to the door!'

'He sounds as though he's better already,' McCall said as Ballard opened the door.

As Peckard saw who his visitors were he gave a relieved sigh.

'God, I thought it was another of them damn women. They keep comin' to visit me. Keep comin' to sit with me so I won't get lonely. Honestly it's enough to drive a man loco.'

Ballard leaned against the end of the bed whilst McCall dragged a chair from against the wall and perched himself on it. Peckard scratched his head and cleared his throat.

'Hell, you don't want to listen to my moaning,' he said. 'I sure am glad you boys got back. How'd it go?'

The old man listened in silence as Ballard gave him a complete report on what had happened. When the Texan had finished Peckard remained silent for a while.

'You give Dicken a proper burial?! he asked.

McCall nodded. 'Wasn't fancy,' he said. 'I don't think the old feller would have wanted anything fancy.'

They spent a while discussing the recent events. Then McCall brought up something that had been at the back of his mind ever since Ballard and him had talked it over on the ride back to Gunner Creek.

'Sheriff,' he began in a tone that caused Peckard to glance at him sharply.

'Something bothering you, boy?' Peckard asked.

Ballard said, 'I reckon I know what Jess is going to say. We had a talk when we were riding in and . . . '

Peckard held up a hand. He nodded his head slowly.

'Don't bother,' he said. 'I can guess. You reckon you've done all the badge-toting you want for now, huh?' He gave a sharp sigh. 'Somehow, I hoped I might persuade you to stay on. This town could use a good hand to keep the law.'

'It has a good hand,' McCall told him. 'Once your leg heals up you'll be okay.'

'Thanks for the compliment, Jess, but hell, I ain't too good at the job anymore.'

'You damn sure were fine when we took on Temple's crew. I hate to think what the result would have been if you hadn't been there.'

Ballard nodded, said, 'Jess is right. 'You don't have to worry any about not being good enough. You get yourself a young feller who wants to make the law his life and you'll be better off than if you had a couple of saddle tramps like Jess and me.'

'I like you too,' McCall said. 'He puts it a funny way, Sheriff, but he's right. I ain't cut out to settle down anywhere for long. After a while I get itchy feet. I just like to drift. Come the day I'll settle but not yet.'

Peckard held out a hand and the Texans removed the badges from their shirts and handed them to him.

Peckard gazed at the tin stars for a while.

'One of these does sort of tie a man down, don't it.' He smiled. 'To tell you the truth I always wanted to see what was on the other side of the hill. Guess I left it too late.'

Ballard caught McCall's eye and nodded towards the door. McCall rose from his chair

'I better go get cleaned up,' he said. 'See you later, Sheriff.'

Peckard glanced up. He asked, 'When you leaving?'

McCall shrugged. 'Maybe tomorrow. We'll drop in before we go.'

Peckard nodded and lay back on his pillow. Ballard followed McCall out into the corridor, closing the door of the room behind him.

'I sort of expected something like that,' McCall said.

Ballard took a deep breath. 'Yeah,' he said.

The desk clerk appeared at the head of the stairs. He saw the Texans and

190

came across to then.

'Your water will be ready in a few minutes, Mr. McCall.'

'Okay, slim,' McCall said and turned towards his room.

Ballard said, 'You'd better put a few gallons on to boil for me.'

'Yes, sir, right away, Mr. Ballard.'

Later they both made their way to the Bonanza Restaurant for a meal. Connie Ward had heard they were back and she came from behind the counter and over to their table as they sat down.

'Hi!' she said as she straightened the blue tablecloth. 'My, don't we all look dandy.'

'We had a bath all on account of because we were coming here,' McCall told her.

'Well, it was worth it. I do declare you both look almost handsome.'

'Only almost,' Ballard said, 'is all I ever hear.'

'You boys hungry?' Connie asked.

'Sort of,' McCall replied.

'Wait a few minutes and I'll put that

right,' she told then.

Within five minutes they were eating their way through large, thick steaks, fried potatoes and eggs, followed by apple pie, and three pots of hot black coffee.

McCall finally put down his cup and leaned back in his chair. He glanced across at Connie who had joined then at the table.

'If this place caught fire right now I sure enough would burn up with it. Man, I never ate so much in a long time.'

Ballard gave a contented sigh and refilled his cup.

'Thank you, ma' am, for a wonderful meal,' he said.

'You are welcome, sir,' Connie said. Changing the subject she said, 'I went to see Ernie a while back and he told me you were in town. He told me what happened. And about Dicken. I'm so sorry.'

'So are we,' McCall said. 'If it hadn't been for Dicken I don't think we would have caught them.'

'Ernie said you're both leaving.'

'Ain't anything to keep us,' Ballard said.

Connie glanced up as someone came into the restaurant.

'Customers,' she said. Before she left them she said, 'You call in before you go.'

McCall nodded. 'Will do.'

'Just what are we going to do when we leave?' Ballard asked.

McCall shrugged his wide shoulders. 'It's a big country out there,' he said. 'Plenty big enough to keep us occupied until we decide.'

'Sounds reasonable,' Ballard said.

And so it was . . .